# The Ghost of Christmas Threeve

© 2024 Jon Lymon

ALSO BY JON LYMON:

The Diamond Rush
Last Night at the Stairways
The Wronged
A Dead Chick and Some Dirty Tricks
A Big Bluff and Some Green Stuff
A Killing Spree and Some Bloody Zombies
The Zombie Cop
Flying Ant Day
Last Writer Sitting / Only a Tool
The Pub Gardeners

# The Ghost of Christmas Threeve

# Chapter 1:
## A Man Soon to be Haunted

Nick Crosby begins this story employed and looking forward to Christmas. But by the second chapter, his job will be gone and with it his enthusiasm for the festive season and life itself. And by chapter three, he will have been visited by a ghost who'll offer him a chance of a reprieve which won't turn out quite as anyone imagines.

And that's when this story really gets Christmessy. And no, that's not a typo.

But first, let's see happy Nick, or Crosby as I'll call him from now on, at home on Christmas Eve morning, spreading butter thickly upon a slice of just-popped wholemeal toast in his state-of-the-art kitchen, eating before walking to his local South London train station with his son, Kyle, who is now old enough to walk back from the shop in the station alone.

Kyle has hatched a plan to buy Christmas presents for his father and mother (Marie) for the first time, from the stationers on the station concourse, using money given to him by his parents as he's too young to work. It's the thought that counts, though.

"Byeeee," they both called out to Mum/Marie as they departed the house, she busy in the spare room art studio in their impressive, expansive and expensive suburban four bedroom home where, in between taking out her frustrations on canvas, she created beautiful portraits of family members and celebrities, some of which she sold online. Or used to.

Once outside with his son, Crosby commented on the mildness of the temperature as he and Kyle strolled to the station, father aware that his offspring nearly matched his five-eleven inches of height, and bemoaning another year about to pass without a sniff of a white Christmas.

"The last one I can remember was 1981," Crosby told Kyle. "When I was about your age."

Given that Kyle was exactly twelve, give or take a few months, that takes care of Crosby's age for you.

"I remember seeing Santa's footprints in the snow, leading from the back gate across the garden to the back door of your grandparents' house," Crosby said, enthusiastically.

"Dad, I don't believe in Santa anymore, so there's no need for the lies."

"It's not lies," Crosby insisted. "Santa existed back then. There were wellington boot footprints in the snow, and no one in our house wore wellies that big."

Father and son talked some more about father and son things and reached the station in seven minutes, Crosby walking his son to the stationer's entrance, a small shop with cards, wrap and enough choice of tat for Kyle to get them both something he hoped they'd like and he'd feel good about giving.

They said their goodbyes and Crosby headed through the barriers down the ramp onto Platform 4 to wait for a train that was never on time and wasn't about to change the habit of a lifetime just because it was Christmas Eve.

"See you at lunchtime," Crosby called back, remembering their restaurant booking. He had no idea if his son heard him, and thought how quickly Kyle had grown up to now be old enough to walk home alone from here.

Seven minutes, that's how long the walk from house to station took. Crosby had walked it a million times. He'd give Kyle ten to do his shopping, and in seventeen minutes, he'd text Marie to check he'd got back home OK.

That Crosby had made no mention of the weight upon his mind that morning was no surprise. That I have made no mention of it until now is perhaps a little more surprising, but I need you to like Crosby as he has a challenging day ahead, and I really don't want you saying 'serves him right,' or words to that effect. Not yet anyway.

So please look upon him as the good father he is, off to work to earn money to support his family. Yes, he's planned to spend some of his income on a round of drinks at lunchtime before the restaurant, to celebrate the festive season with colleagues and to give thanks for the birth of the baby Jesus. And for the fact that he was in the employ of a company that gave all its employees Betwixtmas off as free holiday.

Exactly seventeen minutes after the goodbye while he sat on a train (the fact that he found a seat evidence that it was emptier than usual), Crosby texted his wife and gripped his phone awaiting the reply which was not instantly forthcoming. Ten more minutes passed during which time Crosby allowed himself to consider how he'd feel when the good news he was expecting came through just before midday.

Another ten minutes of daydreaming passed, during which Crosby dismissed thoughts of his son encountering bullies or thieves on his walk home. He disembarked, still gripping his phone and seriously considering not merely texting but calling his wife as he took the stairs up from the platform at City Thameslink to street level.

The lack of chill in the London air Crosby walked through up High Holborn from the station was made up for by a nagging wind and spitting rain. White Christmases in London had been replaced by grey for several years in a row now.

Weather beaten faces stared up at him as they crouched outside the newsagent, holding out half eaten polystyrene cups in the hope Crosby would fill them with festive cheer in the form of coin or better still notes. But his mind was elsewhere. He'd been promised a decision about his internal application to take on a senior developer role before the end of the year. And this being the last working day of the year, that decision had to be conveyed today, or else his bosses were a bunch of liars.

"Spare some change?" came the quietly desperately pleas from street level, dirty overcoats and holey jeans failing to afford their wearers the warmth their struggling bodies needed. Yes, this was hardly the coldest Christmas on record, but a life outdoors plays havoc with the heart, forcing it to work overtime to keep everything functioning.

"Please, sir."

No one calls me sir yet, Crosby thought to himself, but they soon might have to if the promotion that was his by rights became a reality.

"Just a few pence, sir. I take plastic, please."

Crosby saw a dirtied hand pull out a card reader and shook his head at the cheek of the homeless and raised his brow level as close to his hairline as he could safely get.

"If you can afford that machine, you can afford to get off your backside and do some work like the rest of us," Crosby said without slowing his walking pace, moving too fast to hear the reply which he presumed, correctly, would be laden with expletives.

As well as good news about his future, Crosby was also looking forward to lunchtime drinks with his colleagues where he'd reveal his big news, with the alcohol he'd swiftly consume then to be soaked up by the meal with his wife and son at their favourite restaurant, La Spatchas back down by City Thameslink station, this being the sixth year in a row they'd made a Christmas Eve reservation there, which now made it a family tradition.

He pulled out his phone which he'd kept hidden while walking past the homeless. Where was his reply from Marie telling him Kyle was safely home? Had those bullies…

Before the drinks and the meal, Crosby had a morning of 'work' to negotiate, the word in inverted commas for good reason as it was unlikely much hard graft would be undertaken by anyone in the office this close to the holiday season.

Crosby's field of work may seem of little interest and relevance at this point, given that I've already served warning that his job is to be lost - before the clock strikes midday to be precise. But his field of expertise will actually prove vital to the telling of this story. And despite appearances to the contrary, Crosby is wracked with guilt about his career and the direction in which it's heading. If he wasn't, there'd be no story to tell. Suffice to say at this point, his work involved computers and the internet and helping new businesses automate their processes to save time and money and eliminate human error.

The open plan office of Solarvecchi Zotte AI, (for that was the name of the company Crosby worked for), was sparsely populated this Christmas Eve, as many had sensibly booked the day off well in advance. But the top brass demanded a skeleton staff be in place in the run-up to Christmas. And because Crosby had exhausted his supply of days off much earlier in the year, he was fated to being one such bone in the skeleton, perhaps the thigh bone, the biggest but not necessarily the most important. That had to be the spine surely, or the skull? It was something he and the colleague he sat next to - Terry Brown – debated for ten minutes after Terry had greeted his arrival with a knowing, 'Better now?'

wink and a friendly pat on the back, Crosby immediately realising his colleague was referring to the hangover Crosby had been sporting (and disguising with mixed success) since the office party two nights previously.

"It's terrible what ageing does to good, honest, drinking men," said Crosby, waiting for his computer to start up, he and Terry having agreed that the skull was the most important bone in the body as it protected the brain, without which there was no life, no conversation, no tea or coffee, no nothing.

Crosby checked his phone. Marie had finally replied. Kyle was safely home. Now he could relax a little more and concentrate on preparing himself for news about his application for a promotion. Whistling the tune to *O Come All Ye Faithful*, Crosby offered to make tea, not coffee, knowing Terry would refuse as he drank coffee, not tea.

And so Christmas Eve morning passed as was its wont, without a hint of what was to come. So let's fast forward to what was to come, so it comes all the earlier, emails arriving in every inbox simultaneously with multiple pings.

"What's this?" Terry asked. "Season's greetings from on high? The top brass announcing the return of our long-lost Christmas bonus?"

Crosby opened his email with eager anticipation. This was it. The news he'd been waiting for. A pay rise pending, surely. A new year of new opportunity at a new level with more meetings, responsibilities and powers.

And that's when the hush descended as the information in the email was read, re-read, and digested.

People stared at their screens. Crosby actually considered smashing his.

"What sort of company fires half its employees on Christmas Eve?" he quietly asked his monitor.

Turns out that Solarvecchi Zotte AI, with whom Crosby had been employed for six years, had become precisely the kind of company to sack half its people the day before what for many constituted the happiest day of the year.

One of the girls at another table burst into tears, consoled by the mass of white tissue she always kept on her desk, comforted by another girl with even more white tissue.

Crosby peered over to Terry, whose ashen expression told Crosby he'd received a similarly worded message from the CEO.

They both looked up to see the female security guard who had nothing to say for herself standing in the doorway to the office, saying nothing but looking ready to escort the fired from the premises and to lay into anyone who wanted to destroy company property.

"Which half of me are you sacking?" Crosby called out in the direction of the corridor that housed the offices of the firm's top brass. "Cos if it's the left half, I can handle it."

What any of this has to do with Crosby getting embroiled in a ghost story may not be immediately obvious at this stage, but bear with. And know that Terry Brown spat on his screen, grabbed his bag and marched toward that previously mentioned corridor to find said corridor blocked by hired security help, three burly males strong, with little neck to display, even less to say for themselves, and smiles that lacked genuine heart.

"There's no point talking to them anyway," Crosby called over to Terry. "They'll only blame it on the firm's overbearing overheads, or their demanding shareholders or the need for efficiency savings. Always the efficiency savings."

Of the other eight skeleton staff in the office, five faced a similar fate as Crosby and Terry, leaving three unscathed and feeling guilty about it. The CEO had sent the emails en-masse just before lunch, catching his victims unawares minutes before Terry had planned to propose a pint or twelve in The Anchor public house to celebrate the impending anniversary of the birthday of the baby Jesus. Those email pings that had sounded all over the open plan office now reminded Crosby of fragile baubles slipping from the branches of an artificial Christmas tree and hitting bare ground. The impact of those messages shattered egos, stunning those beginning to wind down at the end of a busy year. For the unfortunate, Christmas had been ruined before it had begun.

Crosby read his message thrice, checking it was addressed to him and hadn't been sent by mistake. There was his name at the top followed by copy with a tone cold and to the point, basically giving him strict orders to step away from his workstation within thirty minutes, pack up his stuff and leave the building in an orderly fashion never to return. No one wanted the police involved, but damage to company property would ensure the police got involved.

Crosby had instinctively deleted the message then retrieved it from the trash to re-read it, before deleting it again. There must have been something psychological behind him doing that, but precisely what that was escaped him.

He thought about complaining to HR who were based on the floor below before realising they would have likely drafted the message before getting the CEO to OK and send it.

Crosby wanted to leave via the CEO's office upon whose desk he planned to visit a urination, or at least deposit a wad of spittle, until he saw the security guards blocking the aforementioned corridor, trouble clearly anticipated, defences defiantly posted. None of the disenfranchised had a chance of getting anywhere near sharing a parting V-sign or profanity-fuelled exit message with the fattest cats in the building. The ones who'd nobbled their futures by giving the green light for HR to wield the axe.

The silent female security guard watching Crosby was joined by two of the other three heavies and together they escorted the seven former staff down the stairs and out of work, while the remaining three wondered whether they now had to stay in the office all day as a show of gratitude for still having a job to come back to in the new year.

"Christmas should be a time for bonuses and Secret Santas," Crosby called back up the stairs, his voice echoing off hard, unfeeling stairwell walls. Those who trod the steps of doom alongside him clapped in agreement in between their snivels, sobs and curses.

The entrance to the floor below – home to HR – was guarded by more security, two strong and muscular physiques blocking the doorway. Terry and Crosby knew there was no chance of them getting to wish whoever in HR had drafted that email a Merry Christmas.

A further guard held open the entrance door at ground level, through which the redundant marched in single file, out of the place that once afforded them work. Crosby stopped to shake hands with Leni, the Maltese Office Manager who sat down there in all weathers, greeting arrivals with a smile, always happy to talk life and horse racing with Crosby.

"Today?" Leni said incredulous. "They sack you today?"

Crosby nodded. "All seven of us. In one fell swoop."

Leni shook his head in disbelief.

"Goodbye, my friend," Leni said, tears in his eyes, real warmth in his handshake, his other hand gripping Crosby's shoulder.

Crosby nodded his thanks and followed the others out into the open of the street, rejection taking hold of his mind and body, suddenly sensing the weight of redundancy hanging heavy on his shoulders like Santa's sack, of being surplus to requirements like the giblets of a turkey.

"I'm suggesting we pub it for more than one," Terry suggested, and five of the six fellow disenfranchised agreed.

Let it be said that the other, our very own Nicholas Crosby, felt a sore temptation and natural compulsion to join them, but the old adage *one is too many and ten never enough* rang too true for him. He also knew that had he joined his colleagues in the drowning of sorrows, the topic of conversation would inevitably drift to his indiscretion at the Christmas Party two nights previously – an indiscretion with someone in the office who happened to be one of the lucky three remaining in employment with Solarvecchi Zotte AI, and whom I'm still not ready to tell you about.

Plus, if he goes and gets drunk, this story has precisely zero chance of developing into the ghost tale promised earlier.

So, let us all be thankful that Crosby did the right thing for once and stuck to the original plan, hatched the night before this nightmare of a day. A plan that he knew must be honoured, but could now ill afford to honour.

Goodbyes were said, hugs exchanged, New Year meet-ups arranged when they'd pick the bones out of their situation and seek their revenge, a dish best served cold after Christmas, like Boxing Day turkey sandwiches.

"We're not letting them get away with this," Terry decreed. "We've all done some great work this year and there's precisely zero excuse for these lay offs."

It was then that Crosby and Terry simultaneously remembered something. Both looked back to the building's entrance, blocked by a security guard. They both turned to face each other and grimaced in despair. They needed to get back into the office and onto the system. But it was too late.

Crosby shook his head and salutations of *Merry Christmas* were delivered and received between the group with less relish than would and could and should have been the case.

"Terry Christmas, Merry," Crosby shouted at Terry, not for the first time that December.

"Have a shite Christmas, Bing," Terry replied, also not for the first time that December.

They shot each other the offensive finger like close colleagues ought to and Terry led the others pubwards, allowing us to move on to the next stage of this story, which starts with Crosby watching his former colleagues walking pubwards, wishing he could follow, such was the taste for ale he had in his mouth, haunted by the thought that he and the others would never all share the same office space again.

He took a deep breath of Central London pollution and noted the prevailing mild conditions. Despite the relative warmth, his innards felt a chill, a cold emptiness and loneliness that he ought not to be feeling on this most festive of days. He trod the dank pavement east, in the same direction Terry had led the others, but he didn't detour right down Chancery Lane to the pub. Instead, he kept straight, heading back toward City Thameslink where La Spatchas would be opening ready to lure lunchtime trade, looking down at his feet, missing the joy and anticipation on the faces of people he passed walking west up to Oxford Street with empty bags they planned to fill with last-minute tat.

Marie and Kyle were waiting outside the restaurant as arranged, wrapped in woollen scarves and hats against a cold that hadn't materialised. Both instantly sensed all not being well with Crosby.

"What's up?" his wife asked.

"I'll tell you when we get home."

"Home? We're here for lunch."

Crosby shook his head at his wife and put his hand on his son's shoulder. "Sorry, Kyle, I'm going to have to cancel."

"What?"

"I'm not in the mood. Will explain all when we get home."

"I don't think so," Marie said, grabbing Crosby by his arm. "At the very least I think we deserve an explanation now, here, having travelled all this way at your behest, for a lunch appointment that a matter of a few hours ago you told us you were looking forward to."

"Things have changed. It's beyond my control." Crosby could see the hurt on their faces. Felt something similar in his gut, the rage building to such an extent, the temptation rose to return to the office and urinate over his CEO as well as his desk.

"We're not going anywhere until we get an explanation," said Marie, holding firm in the centre of the pavement, Kyle standing by her side, as last-minute shoppers and alcohol hunters detoured around them.

Crosby walked on a few paces before stopping and turning, tears in his eyes, voice breaking.

"I've lost my job. I thought I was getting a promotion today, but I've been fired," he shouted, throwing his hands in the air like someone casting confetti at a wedding. Only no confetti. And certainly no wedding. This was a divorce. "Half of us have gone. They sacked half the company on Christmas Eve. We're all being replaced by machines."

# Chapter 2:
## In Which The Falling Apart Continues Apace

The miserable silence of the journey home via train and bus is not something I shall inflict upon ye, dear reader. After all, this has been billed as a ghost story, yet so far, you will note no sign of an apparition. All in good time. Suffice to say it's important to know that Crosby received a good deal more sympathy from his significant others on the journey home as he filled them in on the details of events in the office that morning.

"Would you really have taken a leak on his desk, Dad?" Kyle asked, enthralled by that bit of the story.

"I don't know, son," came the reply. "Sometimes when you need to go most of all, they're the times you can't go at all."

"There's stuff in the freezer we can have when we get home," Marie offered helpfully, trying to change the subject. "It won't be restaurant standard but needs must."

Crosby stared out at grey South London passing him by, unexceptional weather on what would have been an unexceptional day had it not been Christmas Eve and the day he'd been made redundant.

The stiff upper lip of coping his wife and child demonstrated strained Crosby's heartstrings to their limit, like elastic bands a millimetre from snapping, his son burying his head in his mobile phone to hide his disappointment at not continuing the family eat-out tradition. Crosby eyed his son's mobile with newfound distaste, considering it something that might have to go unless he quickly found alternative employment which would not be easy. How much was Kyle's monthly bill anyway? How many free texts did he get? Was he contract or pay as you go? Receipts would need reviewing now.

Having hatched a plan with Marie the night before to catch a taxi home from the station after the restaurant, and having made the mistake of promising Marie as much, having to wait in line for the cheaper bus a few hours earlier than planned rankled, especially as he received a text pic from Terry showing everyone merry and drinking and confirming they'd all agreed skull first, spine second, ribs third, and that Solarvecchi Zotte AI needed to go down.

Standing on the lower deck of the sweaty bus happened to be the only option, upstairs too much of a risk around these parts with the young and surly occupying the seats, often with their feet and even more often while partaking of illegal substances.

When someone swaying downstairs close to Crosby started singing *O Come All Ye Faithful* to the tune of *Silent Night*, that was the final straw for Marie who rung the bell a stop early and they disembarked.

As they walked home, Crosby feared for this Christmas already, and it hadn't officially started. The strain on his heartstrings reached a peak as Marie led them into a home full of the colour and shine of a Christmas to come. Walls silvery and gold with tinsel, the new tree artificial but genuinely tall, the tallest ever in a house of Crosby's at seven foot plus the fairy, branches laden with yet more tinsel, its tips hung with baubles. It had all seemed so bright and hopeful that morning. Now it all sickened Crosby to the core, the cost of it all, the fake glitz, symptoms of the commercialisation of the world, much of the joy purchased on Crosby's almost maxed-out credit card, and all to be repaid in February, with the means of repayment now taken away.

He didn't need to raid the cupboards to know they'd be overflowing with food, the freezer working overtime to keep its contents ready for the feast to come. Perhaps they could ration it all, make it last until February. Turkish Delight on Pancake Day. Finish the Christmas pudding on Valentine's. They needn't shop again until spring, except for bread and milk and the other essentials. Now, that was a plan that relieved some of the strain on Crosby, but only momentarily.

He soon felt suffocated, ashamed to be there in his own home that never felt his due to its crippling mortgage and the ridiculously high price of everything, unable to provide the joy his family desired and deserved. Everywhere he turned spoke of expenditure he could ill afford. The crackers, the drinks, and then the small matter of all of the presents.

"Stuff's going to have to go back," he whispered to Marie in a daze after Kyle had left the lounge. "We can't afford it."

Marie turned to him frowning. "Nothing's going back. You can't take food and drink back to the shop," she reminded him. "The butchers won't take the turkey or pigs in blankets back. The garden centre won't have the tree or the decorations."

Crosby's thoughts turned to the gift he'd hidden in his bedside table, the annual token of his love and appreciation for the wife who'd backed him throughout a tough year during which, for the first time in years, cracks had appeared in Crosby's mental state, requiring extended time off during the early summer for mental exhaustion. He'd struggled to get out of bed, on the train, off the train, into the office, out of the office, back into bed. His brain felt full, no more room at the inn and yet the demands of work remained as constant as the guilt.

The project he was working on had serious ramifications beyond the four walls of the office. But the profits it would generate for the top brass within those walls? Astronomical.

Was his extended absence and patchy performance during the year the reason why his name found its way onto today's list of the seven expendables?

"Think of Kyle, Nick. Think of your son. He's only twelve. Don't spoil this for him."

"I don't know what to do, Maz. It's hit me hard. Out of the blue. First time for me, redundancy. It's awful. And I know he's twelve. I was there at his birth."

She embraced him. "Couldn't your bosses wait until the new year to share the bad news?"

Crosby pulled away. He didn't want a discussion. Not even action. Didn't know what he wanted. His thoughts turned to the wrapped computer games for Kyle, three at fifty quid a pop, and to the even more expensive bike due to be hidden behind the lounge curtains later that night.

"It'll break his heart if he doesn't get anything to open tomorrow morning," Marie told him.

"You think I don't know that?"

"We'll manage. You can look for something else in the new year. We've got funds to tide us over."

"Not for long. Two months tops. And I'm not so sure there'll be many other jobs. Not in my sector. Not anymore. The machines will take over."

Marie spotted the signs of Crosby's tension returning., his fists clenched, complexion pale. "Go upstairs for a bit," she advised. "Have a lie down. A sleep will make you feel better. We can watch Basil Rathbone later."

He took a deep breath. Scanned the lounge, the decorations reflecting the house lights, the tree lights now on and pulsing, costing electricity that he'd never worried about paying for before this year when the prices had risen at an incredible rate.

Another deep breath.

We need Crosby to get out of that room now. It's time for the ghostly part to begin.

And thankfully, there he goes.

# Chapter 3:
## Christmas Eve Takes A Ghostly Turn

Upon reaching his bedroom, Crosby reflected on how bedrooms never showed any signs of Christmas. They were decoration free zones, in his house anyway, offering no clue that this was a special time of year. The same layout and décor all year round. No tinsel or lights. And yet the bedroom had such an important role to play in the festivities as, in his house anyway, it was the room in which many of the presents were hidden.

Glad this year's crop were out of his sight if not off his troubled mind, Crosby looked for something to hit, and settled on the top left bedpost of his rather old-fashioned but somewhat valuable mahogany bed, his booted foot taking its rounded top clean off. It had always been loose that bedpost and finally this was the day of the beheading. Crosby watched it roll along the bedroom floor and bang into the wardrobe door.

Not feeling much better for that act of moderate violence, Crosby flopped onto his bed face first, the duvet cold against his skin, feet dangling over the precipice of the mattress. This was not the Christmas Eve he'd envisaged yesterday, even this morning. Oh, how the actions of others could have such a devastating impact on the lives of others. His life. Such power to adversely impact others should not be granted to anyone, anytime of year, but especially today of all days. He, Marie and Kyle should be ordering dessert now at the restaurant, having chatted about which Basil Rathbone and Nigel Bruce *Sherlock Holmes* adventure film they'd watch when they got home, maybe after Kyle experienced his first taste of alcohol, an important concession to adulthood a parent should make on the year their offspring accepts that Santa wasn't, isn't and never will be a thing. Crosby knew it was time to respect that his son was growing up. An advocaat and lemonade wouldn't hurt. Reminded Crosby of his first drinking Christmas.

Sitting up on his bed, he opened the beside cabinet, pulled out his diary (at least a quarter thicker than it had been in January now that he'd written entries on most of its pages), and the old school travel alarm clock behind which he'd stashed a box wrapped in peach paper and gold ribbon. Ladies and gentlemen, this year's last present to be opened on Christmas Day. Never included in the main opening ceremony, this gift represented the ultimate him to her.

Heart-wrenching, he pulled the ribbon and released the knot. Stopped. Got up. Checked the door to the bedroom was shut. Sat back on the bed. Ripped off the paper to reveal the dark red casing. Reached back into the cabinet and pulled out the paper receipt. He always kept gift receipts as Marie could never hide her disappointment if she didn't like a gift, although it had been four years since Crosby had got it so wrong that he needed to action a refund. He couldn't afford to get this year wrong.

He wrapped the receipt around the box and slid it back into the cabinet, throwing the wrapping paper under the bed. Then he laid down on the bed and breathed deeply.

Close to tears, he reflected on how the magic of Christmas had gone. Completely disappeared. Kyle being a believer had rekindled the flame for the last twelve years, but now that was gone too. Like his job and his hope and his enthusiasm.

Although he wanted the promotion and the extra money that came with it, he also knew there was a price to pay - an increase in guilt about the work he was doing. Nothing illegal of course, but the ethics of it were cloudy at best, the tech so new and vast, no legislation had yet been enacted to curtail its spread. He and Terry had talked plenty about what they were doing, most days happy to take the money it afforded them. But some days one or other woke up feeling guilty, and it took one to persuade the other that they had nothing to feel guilty about. After all, they were just doing their jobs.

Thinking of work led Crosby to dwell on his bad behaviour at the Christmas party which you are yet to find out about. And it's still not time to tell you, although it won't take a genius to work it out. In the meantime, he rolled onto his right side on his mattress to face the window and then onto his left to face the bedroom door. Neither view soothed his tortured soul.

Unbearable discomfort. Unliveable guilt. He was both fraud and failure. What was the point of him being there? The work he'd done promised to visit misery on millions. More people than he could picture, more people than he'd ever met in his entire life. But closer to home, the loss of that work promised to visit misery upon his wife and child this Christmas. Marie and Kyle would have a happier Christmas without him. A brighter future, if his life insurance policy was anything to go by.

That was the answer right there. Take the misery maker out of the equation and you're left with happiness.

He flung his legs off the bed and assumed a sitting position.

As he did so, he sensed the bedroom change colour from a pale grey/blue to a vivid yellow/orange like the sun making a rare December appearance. He turned back to the window to confirm no break in the slate grey sky. The source of the light was in the room at the end of his bed where, unless he was very much mistaken, which he wasn't, the bedpost at the left foot end was spinning on its axis, wood chippings flying off and hitting the walls, wardrobe and carpet.

Crosby watched fascinated until the spinning slowed to a stop and he saw that the bedpost had taken on the shape of the face of an old man, forehead lined, hair receded, chin jutting, teeth crooked.

It took a few seconds for the man's eyes to stop spinning and for him to look straight at Crosby who stared back in disbelief.

"So, you think you've got it bad, huh?" The voice was well spoken, slow, croaky, the lips performing impressively to move in synch with the sound.

*Great, a bedpost that talked,* was Crosby's first thought.

He looked around to check he was awake. Check. And this was his bedroom? Check. And he had a pulse? Check.

He stared at the chiselled apparition, features sharp yet crudely carved. "I don't know who you are," Crosby told him. "A stress hallucination, I think. I had one earlier in the year. A cushion came to life and started talking to me, although there was no face."

The old ghost spied the broken bedpost by the wardrobe.

"You killed my brother," he uttered with contempt. "You chopped his head off."

Crosby looked down at the beheaded bedpost.

"Carry on talking rubbish, mate, for as long as you like. I know what this is."

"You have no idea what this is. I very much am here and you are very much there, wasting away, wallowing in misery on this merriest of days."

"Yeah, well, excuse me if I don't partake in the merriment. Being merry costs money, and that's something I don't have access to anymore."

"What are you talking about? You've been handsomely paid for your work for six years."

That got Crosby thinking that he must be due some sort of statutory redundancy pay, something he vowed to talk to Terry about during the Betwixtmas break before they went back. . . .

And then Crosby felt the slump as he realised there was no going back, that this break was permanent.

"Know this," said the bedpost, reasserting its presence. "You are not in quite the pickle you imagine yourself to be."

"Easy for you to say when you're just a head on a bed. No money worries. Nothing. No job to lose. Family to support. Who are you anyway?"

"I've a bed to support and I'm the post that's the ghost of the Christmas you fear most," said the post, poetically, in a manner that suggested he'd delivered that line many times before.

Crosby looked around the room for something he could throw at the post and thought about kicking it so it could join its brother in oblivion.

"Is violence really the answer?" the post said calmly. "Is that how you've taught your son to behave?"

Crosby was getting more concerned. Now this thing had the ability to read his thoughts, as well as talk and move.

"What do you want?" Crosby asked. "Why are you here?"

"I've a job to do. Like I said, I want to show you the Christmas you fear most."

"I'm living it right now."

The bedpost spun and Crosby saw the face depart, returning the mahogany to its regular inanimate smoothness. Crosby scanned the room to see where the face had gone and saw it in the folds of the brown shirt he'd hung on the wardrobe door, ready to wear tomorrow.

"This time yesterday, excitement was in the air, was it not?" Crosby's dark shirt said, brightly.

"I'm pretty sure you know what's changed since then," said Crosby.

The face moved from the shirt across the wooden wardrobe door and animated the makeup removal sponge on Marie's dressing table.

"Your wife and son need you to help them enjoy happiness, if only for a few days. It's been a difficult year, has it not? Your wife's career took a turn for the worse, did it not?"

Not something Crosby needed reminding of. "You expect the years to be difficult when you get older," he said. "But thankfully, they pass quicker."

"You wish to let your wife and child down?" the sponge spoke with conviction.

"Of course not."

"But here you are, alone in this room, letting worries about the future cloud the here and now."

"I've got to think about the future. Else we'll all be out on the street."

"Ahh, that is what you fear most."

"Not having a roof over my family's head? Of course I fear it. More than I fear for my sanity talking to a sponge."

"Surely you must know that there are people far worse off than you this very evening and every other evening of the year for that matter."

"Can't you let a man wallow a little in his own misery on the day he lost his job? Surely that's good grounds for wallowing?"

The face returned to the bedpost and spun to look at him. "The self pity of the man who's had life easy."

"Easy? What do you know about life being easy? What do you know about life?"

"Enough to show you a thing or two. Actually three."

"Just do one, mate, I'm not in the mood. I was this morning, then I lost my job on the day I thought I was getting a promotion, and funnily enough that's caused me to lose my appetite for celebrating."

"How many more Christmases do you expect to have?" asked the bedpost.

"What?"

"You are not so young anymore. There is no guarantee."

"There never was. I just didn't know it back then."

"Every Christmas could be your last. You want to spend your last Christmas like this?"

"That's a bit grim isn't it? You're certainly not here to cheer me up, are you?"

"I've been sent to give you a once in a lifetime opportunity that is not afforded to many mortals."

"What? Can this get any worse?"

The eyebrows of the bedpost ghost rose. "Actually, that is precisely why I'm here," he said.

Crosby looked at him, inviting the apparition to tell him more.

"Your day could get worse, or infinitely better. Want to find out?"

"I don't know what you mean."

"I have the power to show you three alternative Christmas Eves to the one you are currently experiencing."

"Why would you do that?"

"You are at the end of your tether. Here's a chance to extend that tether, so you will no longer be at its end."

Crosby sat up, beginning to take this apparition seriously. "You serious?" he asked, confirming that previous assertion.

"You have the chance to re-live this Christmas Eve thrice, and upon the end of the third, you must choose which of the three alternate realities you wish to be your actual reality for the rest of time, and it shall be done."

"You can do that?"

"Of course."

"How?"

"There is much your kind needs to learn about the spirit world."

"Why are you doing this?"

"Because you have been designated an emergency case. Which means there's worry among my bosses that you're on the verge of throwing your life away."

Crosby let that message hang in the air, its truth cutting deep.

"So, you're like my genie offering me my very own groundhog day?" he asked in an attempt to lighten the mood.

"You're not the first to say that, so don't go thinking you're being clever."

"What if I don't like any of these alternate realities?"

"Then you should not agree to take part and I shall take my leave of you here and now."

Crosby's heart sank at the prospect of being left alone in the room with his dark thoughts. He took a look around the bedroom and searched his soul and came back empty handed. The day's events had hit him hard, so had this hardest of years. How easy was it going to be for him to find employment again at his age, with younger people gunning for his job and machines gunning for everyone's job?

Crosby turned to face the bedpost. "Just to be clear, there's three options and I have to choose one, right?"

"Correct."

"And these scenarios..."

"I cannot discuss them as I cannot foresee their nature, only their number."

That didn't settle Crosby's growing nerves.

"But they could be worse or better than this mess I'm in now?"

"Correct."

"How long will it all take?"

"Don't worry about time. You won't miss a thing you don't want to miss."

Crosby replayed that line over in his head. It seemed to make sense but he was more conscious than ever of his heart thumping hard.

"Are there forms to sign, payments to pay, any guarantees of satisfaction?"

The bedpost apparition slowly closed its eyes. Another client with a procrastination problem, it seemed. "None whatsoever. No paperwork. No payments. No guarantees. Are you in? Or shall I leave? I've got other patients... people to see."

Crosby took a deep breath, glossing over the patients reference and thought about Marie and Kyle downstairs and if he should tell them about this before getting involved. Best not, he concluded, and with a little excitement and a lot of tension in his body, he nodded.

And with that, the light in the bedroom faded and Nick Crosby lay back on his bed as directed by the bedpost and before long, his consciousness was lost.

# Chapter 4:
## Alternate Christmas The First

Crosby, like the rest of mankind, had every right to expect to wake up in the same place in which he'd fallen asleep. It's not a lot to ask for. But this isn't that kind of story. After all, if bedposts and shirts on wardrobe doors and makeup sponges on dressing tables can talk, surely a lead character who went to sleep in his warm bedroom can wake to feel his skin freezing and hear the sound of flapping above his head.

A trapped bird, it must be, Crosby thought to himself before he'd opened his eyes. Most likely a robin in the rafters this time of year. Crosby loved the robin, such an unassuming bird and yet so distinctive. *So* Christmas.

He opened his eyes and sat up, discovering blue canvas flapping about his head, and in place of his duvet, a cheap blue sleeping bag, his beige socks poking out of a rip in the far end, toes cold due to exposure to the temperature, it being significant degrees Celsius and Fahrenheit cooler than a room with fully functioning central heating ought to be.

OK, this was weird, Crosby thought, but to be expected after what the bedpost... had he really been talking with a bedpost before falling asleep?

He reached up at the canvas which seemed to be closing in on him as well as moving and touched the top without needing to fully extend his arm. The surface felt flimsy, the walls angular. Unless he was very much mistaken, which he wasn't, Crosby had awoken inside a tent.

"Losers, losers," a voice chanted from the other side of his canvas walls.

Crosby saw shadows framed by lights moving in the distance outside. He sat up and reached for an old pair of boots, waiting neatly next to each other beside his sleeping bag on a crinkled blue groundsheet.

His exposed feet in need of warming, he struggled in the limited space to slip into the boots while trying to answer a few pressing questions, the most pressing of which was 'what was he doing in a tent?' Also pressing: Where was Marie? Certainly not beside him keeping him warm. Where was Kyle? Where was the mahogany bed and where was his house? What had happened to Christmas Eve? And the ghost?

Crosby quickly calculated that answers to these questions would not be found in his current location, so he stooped inside his tent smelling the unwelcome spice of bodily odour as he moved toward the zipped entrance. Not an attractive smell, but an occupational hazard for the camper, the tent dweller, which was the state he now assumed he'd awoken in.

He unzipped the front of his tent and peered out into a chilly night, his breath intermittently clouding his view. Ahead, a streetlamp lit a path that stretched left to right, running parallel with iron railings through which Crosby could see a dual carriageway, on the far side of which were tall buildings, dark save for security lights in a few of the windows. Closer to home, his attention was drawn to a bench in the park under the lamplight on which two male youths passed a bottle back and forth, slugging from it then surrendering.

He stood outside his tent and stretched, noticing first how much his belly had shrunk. Was he wasting away? He felt his ribs protruding from his torso, the first time he'd experienced that since his early teens. Reaching to fondle his chin and ponder his predicament, his hands were greeted by the wiry wool of a beard which further investigation revealed was all over his face and thick enough for birds to consider for nesting.

Marie would go mad, he thought. She hated even a day's stubble on him.

Content that Marie wasn't in the vicinity to launch a complaint, he surveyed his surroundings, his back aching, his eyes seeing more tents lined up under the trees either side of his. Turning a full 360 where he was standing revealed a village of canvas behind him in haphazard lines five, six deep. A community of rough sleepers?

"Oi."

Crosby turned back to see one of the young drinkers striding toward him.

"Yeah, you. Loser," the kid added.

On this day of days, Crosby struggled to argue against the young man's assertion. He remembered the job loss email, the misery of telling Marie and Kyle. Not going to the restaurant. Getting home.

Panicking. Lying down. Wanting to end it all. The face, the face in the bedpost. What was that all about? Had he drunk one too many celebrating the festive season at lunch time? No, he remembered he hadn't touched a drop.

The youth striding toward him evidently had no intention of exchanging presents or pleasantries. Crosby looked for something with which to defend himself from the inevitable attack but came back empty.

"Go back to where you've come from, scum," the youth insisted. As anticipated, the kid swung a punch but drink had poisoned his accuracy and Crosby easily dodged the assault.

'Try that again, and I'll take you down," Crosby threatened, too old to let someone so young get away with something like that.

"What are you doing here, loser?" The youth tried to cover his humiliation with further verbals. "You people are an embarrassment. Haven't you got homes to go to?"

Not having acquainted himself with any of his fellow tent-dwellers, Crosby had no idea if his current situation was a temporary housing arrangement or something more permanent.

Crosby glanced at the second of the two youths, hanging back in the shadows cast by the oaks in the park, perhaps not as drunk or as aggressive as his mate but certainly taller.

"I'm here for the New Year fireworks," Crosby told him. All he could think of in the heat of the moment.

"Bit keen aintcha?"

"Why, how long to go?"

"You been drinking?"

"No."

'You're a week early, mate. And I wouldn't pitch your tent with this bunch of losers. They'll all get moved on by the rozzers before new years. Losers the lot of 'em."

So it was still Christmas Eve. Crosby wasn't sure if that made things clearer or muddied the waters further.

"Where can I get something to drink round here?" Crosby asked. "What pubs are there?"

"I'm not sure you'll get in looking and smelling like that."

"I'll tidy myself up."

"There's the Bear, the Anchor, the George, but they'll all be ticket only tonight, Christmas Eve."

All the names rang familiar, the pubs of his hometown. And now it was all making sense as he looked around. He recognised the dual carriageway. And the tall grey building beyond – the magistrates court. Further to the right, a side road led to the law courts and beyond that the train station. His tent must be pitched in Fairfield Park on the edge of town, the other side of the roundabout from his house. This park was somewhere he'd driven past thousands of times without ever having set foot inside. It was known locally to attract rough sleepers and drug takers who were often one and the same. OK to walk your dog in here during the day and not pick up their deposits. But after dark, owner and dog best keep away.

"I know people who work the doors," Crosby lied.

"So what the hell..."

"Keep the noise down out there will ya."

That was the voice of someone from within one of the other tents in the village. From the rasp in the tone, it sounded like they smoked forty a day and never touched a drop of water.

"Loser," the lad shouted.

Muttering followed from inside the tent, but no one ventured outside to take the matter further.

Crosby shaped to re-enter his tent.

"What you doing?" the youth asked.

"I'm getting changed, ready to go out."

"You got a change of clothes in there?"

Crosby had no idea what he had in there but given its size it was unlikely to harbour a wardrobe of clothing, a rack of shoes, a rain shower with heated towel rail, or a flushing toilet.

"I've got nothing worth nicking mate, if that's what you're wondering."

"You must have some drink?"

Crosby pulled open the flap and invited the youth inside.

"Bloody hell, mate, that's disgusting," the kid said, inhaling then withdrawing.

"Telling me."

"Got any money on you?"

Crosby turned out his pockets. "I don't think the people living in tents are going to be your best target if you're looking to rob people. This is probably a strict hard drug taking neighbourhood."

"I don't mess with that stuff," said the youth backing off. "Don't want to end up unemployed like you lot."

Crosby nodded. "Make sure you keep thinking like that."

The youth wandered back to his friend and Crosby braved the stench of his tent, searching for a change of clothes, discovering nothing but the sleeping bag and a jacket he'd been using as a pillow.

"This is what you think is going to happen to you?"

Crosby struggled to keep his bones inside his skin, such was the violent shock of hearing a voice in his tent and seeing the shape of a face in the creases of the canvas.

"It's you."

"Have you met the neighbours?"

"Not yet. I wasn't planning on borrowing a cup of sugar. Not the ideal pitch this."

"Beggars can't be choosers."

"Is that what I am? You bought me to a scenario in which I'm a tramp?"

"Are you not concerned with why there's so many people camping out here?"

"Are they here for the fireworks?"

"Why don't you ask them? Maybe you will find out they've been here for months."

"Months?"

"Go and ask."

"I'm not feeling very sociable. I'm a bit shy, and there's no bell to ring or door to knock on with a tent, is there? It's all slightly awkward. It's the day I lost my job, remember?"

"No, it isn't. You're forgetting. That was in a different reality."

"What do you mean?"

"I bet some of your neighbours had good jobs once upon a time. Then they lost them. Maybe on Christmas Eve. Maybe before. Maybe it's their fault, they're here. Maybe it's someone else's. Make wrong decisions after losing your job and anyone could easily end up somewhere like this. Especially if you start feeling sorry for yourself, moping around in your bedroom. There's all kinds of reasons why someone could find themselves living out here. But those with reasons to keep going should be looking for a way out, don't you think?"

"What do you mean by that?"

"This is a difficult world you find yourself in now, Nick. And getting out of it won't be easy. I assume you do want to get out of here?"

"I'd love to get out of this stinking tent and these damp clothes."

"I'm afraid I can't sympathise, never having needed clothes. How you get out of this is up to you. You have to find your own path. That's part of the deal. You get to experience a different reality and if you don't like it, well..."

"You mean you can't just transport me somewhere else on demand if I want out?"

"I told you I'm not a genie. It was all in the small print."

"You didn't show me any small print."

"I didn't? Ah. Sorry. I always forget that bit. Mainly because no one ever reads the small print."

"So what do I do? Where do I go?"

"Well, the good thing is you're somewhere you know, so there may be some people you know."

"But how did I get like this? Have I gone back in time, forward?"

The face of the old man faded as the creases in the canvas flattened until the apparition was gone, his parting words "follow your nose" echoing in the night.

Crosby sniffed the air and felt his nose, a little sore and more bulbous than he remembered. And was that a piercing, a sleeper in the right nostril? Marie would go mad.

Getting into the jacket he'd been using as a pillow, Crosby left his tent, zipping it up, wondering if he should take it with him. A lack of rucksack would make that difficult. But did he need the tent? Was it the portal to the next reality? If it wasn't here, would he be stuck in this alternate world forever? The ghost had a lot to answer for, especially with the not mentioning the small print thing, although he was right, no one ever read the small print.

The two drinking kids had gone, that was the good news for Crosby as he exited the tent. The next not-so good news was how hungry he felt. He knew that burger vans plied their trade near the station but burgers equalled money and he'd already established a distinct lack of that. Looking to his right he saw a few shadows shuffling from the tented village toward the east exit of the park and decided to follow them. Within a few steps he smelt the aroma of food wafting in the air from that direction.

A pop-up soup kitchen just inside the east entrance revealed itself, a white caravan with a canopy that opened up one side to reveal a kitchen staffed by a crew of three, an older man and woman who could easily be husband and wife on cooking detail, and a young girl serving who reminded him of the girl who worked in La Spatchas.

An orderly queue of the disorientated sporting dirty woollen hats, non-matching scarves and a variety of thick, sodden clothes had formed outside the soup kitchen where three iron cauldrons were being stirred in turn by the elderly couple while the young girl politely informed the growing queue of those growing hungry that it would only be a couple of minutes before the soup was ready.

"What is it?" someone asked.

"You get a choice," the young girl smiled back. "Chicken, tomato or winter vegetable."

"Must be Christmas," proclaimed the guy first in line. "I haven't had a choice since last Christmas."

Others in the queue nodded knowingly.

The girl smiled and looked at Crosby about tenth in line, a flash of recognition crossing her face, or was that wishful thinking on his part? Crosby looked away, embarrassed to be seen looking like this. As he did so, his eye caught a strange message graffitied in red spray on the pavement: Luddites Live.

That's when a bottle smashed over the head of an old homeless guy in a green beanie standing three in front of Crosby.

Crosby turned to see the kid who had called him a loser earlier laughing. But there was worse to come. His friend, who'd refused to come near the tent in the park, and who had clearly just launched the bottle, was Kyle.

"Kyle!" A stunned Crosby surrendered his place in line to approach his son.

Kyle backed off, looking at him without a hint of recognition.

"How do you know my name?" he asked.

"I gave it to you. Me and your mother decided on it."

Kyle frowned. His friend looked at them both in turn.

"There's definitely a resemblance there, Kyle." He then burst out laughing.

"Your mum's called Marie," Crosby added.

The humour disappeared in an instant from his friend's face.

"How do you know all this?" Kyle was backing away, freaked out as he'd every right to be, Crosby becoming more and more upset by his son's reticence.

"Is this your old man?" the other kid asked, swaying a little.

Kyle shook his head. "Let's get out of here."

"Why did you throw the bottle, Kyle?" Crosby asked.

"I don't want them here. Nobody wants them here." Kyle pointed to the queue then the tents.

The guy standing next to the guy who'd been hit by the bottle stepped forward. "You think any of us wants to be here? You think we wanted our jobs to be stolen by machines, our means of earning a living taken away from us virtually overnight?"

The girl from the soup kitchen dabbed a damp tea towel on the scalp of the bottled man, no blood thankfully, due in part to the thickness of the beanie, but a lump forming.

"Can't you get another job?" Kyle asked.

"Why should I? It's the people who created the machines who should be doing something different, not me."

Kyle turned to Crosby. "My Dad used to work in computers I seem to remember. Before he abandoned me and my mum."

"That was a long time ago," Crosby answered, feeling awkward with eyes on him.

"Most of us used to work with computers," said the other man. "Just not designing tech specifically to take people's jobs away."

Kyle shrugged and shaped to leave.

"Where's your mum, Kyle?" Crosby called out.

Kyle scanned the battered, hairy face in front of him, noting something familiar in the eyes.

"I'm not telling you. Even if you are who you say you are. You left us years ago and I doubt mum wants anything to do with you."

Kyle and his friend ran off toward the train station.

What was he doing out on the streets at this time of night at his age, Crosby wondered. Not even a teenager and already drinking in public, although he was tall enough to pass for a mid to late teen.

Crosby's appetite had vanished, but he rejoined the queue about twenty people further back from being served than he had been and it was twenty minutes before he chose winter vegetable, the cup warm in his hands, the food coating his insides. He made short work of it, tempted to rejoin the end of the queue for another helping until he saw how far it snaked back into the park.

Crosby wandered around side-eyeing the faces, none of which were familiar. One lined and bearded face looked very much like the next.

What to do, where to go? He leant against a lamppost near the east gate.

"Do you remember walking past any of those people today?"

Crosby instinctively jumped toward the exit until he saw the ghost's familiar face carved into the trunk of one of the old oaks.

Crosby took a closer look at the faces all around him. "Which ones?"

"Nick, in your other reality, you walked past all of these people today. Some of them begged you for help and you just walked by."

"I can't stop for everyone."

"You didn't stop for anyone."

"I had things on my mind."

"A promotion? Into a role that would give you the chance to develop more tech to take more people's jobs away?"

"Shut up." Crosby looked around to make sure no one was within earshot. "I got fired, remember."

Crosby sheltered behind the trunk in the shadows and scanned the soup sippers and those waiting patiently in line for their sustenance, not recognising any of them. But then again, there were so many homeless in London, you got so used to seeing them. You can't remember them all.

"You didn't help any of them, did you? Not one."

Crosby looked down into his cup at the remaining cube of carrot and lone pea.

"It's Christmas, and you couldn't find it in your heart to help fellow human beings."

"I've had a bad year, mentally. A lot of money spent on treatment that didn't work. I've spent a lot on Kyle too. And I got Marie a nice watch she wanted. A few thousand quid's worth. I don't spend loads on myself. Drink, maybe, but that's it."

"You had a very well paid job in that world. But you lost it. What do you think will happen if you continue along the path you began to walk in that world?" the ghost asked. Crosby moved away from the tree as a few people hugging cups of soup drifted toward him. "Those thoughts you were thinking on the bed. Would you have gone through with them?"

"A lot of it was heat of the moment stuff. You know, you expect a day to go one way and it takes a completely different turn. That sort of thing gets harder to take the older you get. There's less time left to get to where you want to be."

The ghost nodded almost imperceptibly.

"What are you doing here anyway?" he asked the ghost. "If people see me talking to you. . ."

"They can't see me. They only see you talking to a tree."

"I don't want that."

"You followed your nose. Now it's time to follow your heart."

"My heart's taken a pounding seeing Kyle like that."

"So it should. You deserted him and his mother."

"I'd never leave them, that's not me."

"Clearly in this reality it is you."

"I'd never let it come to this. I'd find something to do. Some way of stopping it getting this bad."

"Seems the employment market isn't great at the moment. The machines must be taking over. And you're responsible for them taking over, aren't you, Nick?"

Crosby looked around, very wary of anyone hearing this kind of talk.

"Maybe the work you were doing led to the loss of your own job. You invented automated tech that, after automating millions of other people's jobs away and causing them to lose their careers, eventually automated your own job, giving you a taste of the misery your work had inflicted on others. That's the reason why you got overlooked for a promotion in the other reality, isn't it?"

"I don't know. They didn't say. Employers don't have to say why they're sacking you. They can do what they like."

"Look around you. I'll wager many of the people here used to work good jobs until they were automated away. Do you want to find out?"

"No."

"You want to tell them what you did for a career."

Crosby shook his head.

"Why? Are you ashamed?"

Crosby looked down at his feet again. "Like you said, that's in a different reality."

"You weren't ashamed of your work while it was earning you a good salary, were you? You didn't care what your tech was costing other people when it was earning you big bucks, putting you in line for a big promotion and making you attractive to younger women in the office. Women like Tamsin."

"That's... I was a different..."

"You knew what you and Terry were doing would put thousands of people out of work, didn't you?"

"I was hired by Solarvecchi Zotte AI to develop automated tech to improve business efficiency."

"And the biggest way a business can improve its efficiency?"

Crosby shrugged.

"Come on. Out with it."

"Cut the payroll," he mumbled.

"What? I can't hear you."

"Cut the payroll," he said loudly. "Paying people represents fifty to sixty per cent of the average firm's expenditure."

"So, replace humans with machines and, hey presto, massive savings on the bottom line."

"It's the way of the world. Every company is doing it."

"Because you gave them the means to do it."

"Not just me. There are thousands of people doing what I do."

"Thousands?"

"Well, hundreds. Maybe thousands."

"A few hundred people like you are getting very well paid to invent technology that takes millions of people's jobs away."

"If not me, someone else would do it."

"I don't care about them. I want to know why you worked a job you knew would destroy lives."

"It was well paid. I've got a mortgage and family to support. There were good benefits."

"Good benefits! Look around you, Nick. What benefits do you see?"

Desperation was writ large on the weather worn faces of the people who sat nearby supping soup from ice white cups and rubbing dirty fingerless gloved hands together, some with shivering dogs at their feet, others with open toed leather boots on their feet.

"You put many of these people here," the ghost continued. "They have no future, no purpose. The skills they learned were made redundant by your inventions. How does that make you feel?"

More of the hungry homeless walked from the tented village toward the soup kitchen, drawn in by the smell.

"If I was so responsible, how did I end up like this then? Why aren't I living in some palace?"

The ghost shrugged. "Like I said, I don't have all of the answers. I'm just trying to help you make the right decisions."

Crosby threw his cup toward the bin. Missed. Stooped to pick up the still warm polystyrene and dropped it in.

"My son, he didn't recognise me. Said I went missing."

"You must remember that you're experiencing a completely different reality."

"I've had enough. I want to go."

"You're not curious about Marie?"

"Of course I am. Do you know where she is?"

"Well…"

The apparition faded into the bark.

"Come on, tell me."

"She's doing OK," said the voice becoming feint. "All things considered."

"Is she still living locally," Crosby shouted

"Yes, in the same…"

And it was gone.

Crosby wasted no time exiting the park and walking toward the town's main roundabout, always so busy with traffic, it was handy they built an underpass.

Of course this was filled with the temporary homes of the dislocated and disenfranchised. Prime real estate compared to the exposed park he'd come from. Down here, pitches were allocated on a first come, first served basis, or at least on the basis of whoever fought the hardest or dirtiest got to live here.

The place reeked of faeces and urine, to be expected given the number of inhabitants. But the police had obviously insisted a pathway be kept clear of tents to allow whoever was foolish enough to venture under here to get to whatever exit they needed to get to.

Crosby walked east to west and did so with great haste, looking straight ahead to his exit, never to the side, not wanting to catch the eye of any of the tent dwellers who may be spoiling for a fight or seeking a pocket to pick, not that his harboured any loot.

He was conscious of faces looking at him, of drinkers pausing their slugging to check out the new arrival, of dirty fingers scissoring gaps in tent flaps to view the source of the noisy footsteps splashing through the pools of piss and vomit.

Crosby's stride was confident enough to get him to the far side of this subterranean hellhole in one piece and he ascended the steps to street level, relief increasing with every step.

His former home was less than half a mile from the roundabout, and it felt strange to return to a neighbourhood he was used to returning to smartly attired and fairly clean shaven every day after work.

His house looked familiar from the outside, a classic frontage of door with windows either side up and downstairs. He paused on the pavement that bordered the small front garden and peered into the living room, the lights warm and welcoming, with a Christmas tree blinking multi-coloured magnificence. Before long, a shadow in the shape of a man rose, walked toward the window and pulled the curtains shut.

Crosby took a deep breath, turned to leave but paused as the ghost's familiar facial form reappeared, warping the glass in one of the windows.

"Outside looking in. Not a great way to spend Christmas, is it?"

"She's not here?"

"She was forced to move out when you left, Nick. Couldn't afford it on an artist's unreliable income."

"Where did she go?"

"Where the council forced her to go."

Crosby's mind flicked to the horror of the rectangular high rises that spouted in the west of the city, many adjacent to the train line that ran from London to Brighton.

"I wouldn't have left her."

"Clearly you did."

Crosby couldn't think why he would have left his family, unless…

"I wasn't unfaithful, was I?"

The ghost's face froze in the glass. "I've multiple clients to see. This is one of my busiest nights of the year."

"For people wanting to end it?"

"Of course. Lonely people see others enjoying themselves and get a sense of what they're missing and end up making stupid decisions."

The first floor window of the house to the left opened, and a guy in his thirties looked down. "Oi, mate, what are you doing? Who are you talking to?"

Crosby realised his situation didn't look good. "I'm looking for someone who used to live here. Marie. Marie Crosby."

The guy nodded. "I remember Marie. She moved out a few years ago. Dunno where. Although last I heard she was working at the old people's home, the Darby and Joan."

"I'll check it out," said Crosby nodding his thanks. "Merry Christmas."

The guy stared at him for a couple of seconds, unable to bring himself to return the yuletide greeting and slammed shut his window before drawing the curtains.

The old people's home was only half a mile from the house and he could avoid the tent underworld under the roundabout to get there. On his way, he crossed the road whenever he saw people approaching on the same side, not wanting confrontation, his feet sore in ill-fitting boots that incessantly rubbed against his heels.

The Darby and Joan was in a fairly pleasant residential area of the town, the wealth of the neighbourhood's inhabitants reflected by the number of festive lights that adorned windows, doors, driveways and fences.

The retirement home had a large parking bay out front, designed to be roomy enough for a London ambulance to pull in and pull out in a hurry. The bay was empty right now, but it was only a matter of time before the next blue flashing visitor pulled up.

Crosby paused at the gate at the end of the pathway and watched a woman quietly close the front door and walk down the few steps into the parking bay. Even from this distance and even though she wore a thick grey bobble hat and thick black glasses, he could tell it was her.

"Marie?"

She stopped suddenly, checked her handbag perhaps for pepper spray or an alarm, considered turning back into the house.

"Don't go. It's me."

"What do you want? How did you know I'd be here?" she asked.

"I went to the house." Crosby could see she couldn't bear to look at him.

"I'm sorry for what happened," he added.

Finally, Marie plucked up the courage to look up, unable to hide her shock at his unkempt appearance.

"What happened to you?" she asked, taking perverse pleasure in seeing him looking so down and dowdy. If he'd been smart and smiley she would have been devastated.

"Life, I guess."

"You got a nose piercing."

"Drunken decision."

"And a beard."

"No choice. No razor or mirror."

"She left you, did she?"

Crosby grimaced internally. So, he *was* unfaithful. That's what caused all this. Had to be Tamsin at work, though he daren't mention her name. What if he was wrong and it was someone else? Marie would think he'd been playing the field.

"Yeah. We drifted apart. Pretty quickly actually."

"Shame."

"How about you? Did you ever meet someone else?"

He couldn't stop himself glancing down at her left hand but didn't have an angle to see her ring finger.

"I met some people, but could I trust them? No way. My trust is damaged. Never to recover."

Crosby stared down at his feet. "I don't know what I was thinking getting involved with her."

"You were thinking you wanted some fun, away from the family with someone younger and prettier."

"I wouldn't say she was prettier, and not much younger either."

"You don't have to say anything. This skin has hardened thanks to you, to the point now that it's virtually impenetrable."

Time for Crosby to change the subject.

"I saw Kyle. He didn't recognise me."

"I'm not surprised. Not sure I would if it wasn't for hearing your voice first."

"How's he doing at school and stuff?"

"Pretty good considering his mum has to work three jobs and there's still not enough to put food on the table or presents under the tree."

"If it's any consolation. . ."

"It won't be."

Crosby nodded to himself and felt the discomfort of standing in a situation he didn't quite know how he got into. From the body language, there was zero chance of Marie inviting him back to wherever she lived for a shave, fresh clothing and a warming glass of Christmas Eve forgiveness.

"Look, I've got to head back, to my place," he said.

"You can't be living near here, surely?" she asked.

"I'm temporarily in town for the fireworks at New Year."

"Already? Are you doing the display?"

"No."

"Oh. It's just that it's been all over the papers that AI tech is being used in this year's show to make it the most eye-popping performance ever."

"I don't read the papers. I just sleep under them. I booked a place near Fairfield Park for Christmas and Betwixtmas."

"Nice is it?"

"Small, very small. And drafty."

"Good. What are you doing for work?" she asked.

"I dunno. I mean, my last contract ended in November and there's still nothing on the horizon."

This was all made-up nonsense, of course, and Crosby wasn't convinced that Marie was buying any of it. Surely she could see from the state of him that he hadn't enjoyed a roof over his head for months.

"But aren't your skills in high demand right now? Everyone's automating everything. I can't switch on the TV or flick through my socials without seeing AI this, AI that."

"Yeah, there's plenty of work around, but I had that mental relapse thing again recently, so I've been forced to take it easy."

"What mental relapse?"

Crosby paused. "It's nothing."

Another awkward pause followed during which Marie's demeanour made it clear she was in no mood to listen to a sob story.

"Did you know that my art market dried up completely once AI started taking over?" she asked him. "Once people could create their own art for free, using tech trained on my and others' copyrighted art, for free, there was no need for me. No way I could make a living."

"I never worked on the art side of AI, I told you that."

"But you were part of that world. Siding with the machines against the people, even though it damaged my livelihood, ruined my passion, devalued my work."

That was a lot for Crosby to take in. "I actually left the AI world years ago," he said. "Why else do you think I look like this?"

"I read about the Solarvecchi Zotte AI takeover, Nick, a few years back. Your name wasn't mentioned. You were long gone from there by then."

"They forced me out."

"Sympathy is in short supply around here."

"Well, I'll say goodbye, then."

The two exchanged a lingering look, the love they once had for each other deeply buried under regret and resentment.

"Here, take this." Marie removed her bobble hat. "You need it more than me."

Crosby wanted to give Marie something back by way of thanks for looking after the son he'd clearly deserted for reasons that still weren't apparent, but he carried nothing of value. Even if he had, its value would have nowhere near compensated for what he'd done to Marie, even if he had the bank balance of one of the top brass at Solarvecchi Zotte AI.

What had happened to Crosby in the intervening six years? He could have done with interrogating Marie further. But her body language spoke of an urge to get away from him and he stepped aside to let her pass, listening to her footsteps fade and then to the rasp in his lungs, feeling the harshness of his flesh, as his hairs stood on end.

So what now?

Questions about his fate still needed answering. Like how did he, a successful tech developer with in-demand coding skills end up smelling like the drains were up? And could he be bothered to find out, when he had an easy way out of here via the ghost?

It should come as no surprise that Crosby took the easy way out, walking back to the park and his odorous tent in which he planned to lie down, fall asleep, drift away and wake up in a new wonderland.

Why Crosby expected his tent to still be in the exact pitch he'd left it in Fairfield Park isn't entirely clear. No one leaving property unattended in most parts of town could realistically expect it to still be there when they returned, even if it was a measly tent that had been urinated upon by strangers multiple times, with an interior that sported an unfriendly odour.

Reaching the park and seeing no tent that answered to the description he saw in his mind's eye, in an ecstasy of panic, Crosby scanned the tented village, sure he wouldn't recognise his tent even if it were right in front of him with a neon sign saying 'I'm your tent, loser', given he'd woken up in it for the first and only time just a few hours ago. The smell he might recognise, but to sample that he'd have to get inside. Who'd let a stranger inside their tent to smell it?

He stood in the park and faced the bench under the lamplight where Kyle and his friend had been drinking. His pitch would have been right where he was standing. And there was no sign nor scent of his tent.

He then became conscious of two men approaching from the direction of the pop-up soup kitchen, neither carrying soup or looking like they slept rough. There was little doubt they were heading for him and Crosby's feet were too sore to run.

They stopped a few feet from him and nodded.

"Interested?"

Crosby shrugged before he realised one of the men was holding out a leaflet headed *Neo Luddite*. Crosby quickly ascertained they were recruiting.

"The revolution's coming, my friend," said the same guy who'd spoken before, the one without the leaflet. "The people who force you to live out here will get their comeuppance. Will you join us?"

Crosby shrugged. "I'm not in town for long. Just here for the fireworks."

"We're in every town. Where are you headed next?"

"West. I'm heading west in the new year. Visiting family."

"Spread the word, my friend, the fightback begins soon, maybe before the year's out. Be ready."

The other guy clearly expected Crosby to take the leaflet which he did, although its A5 size made it nowhere near big enough to sleep under, but it might pass as a snack.

He watched the two men disappear into the fog of night before his thoughts returned to his predicament. Even more disturbing than the loss of his one and only source of shelter in this world was the loss of somewhere he could reconnect with the ghost that had gotten him into this mess.

"Ghost? Where are you, Ghost?" Crosby called out in desperation, the kind of line that gets you strange looks from passers-by who are unfortunate enough to hear you. Fortunately, apart from the two Luddites, passers-by were few and far between in Fairfield Park at this time of night.

Given the ghost's penchant for appearing in objects, Crosby concluded, correctly, that standing in an open space with a smattering of trees was unlikely to be the best place to make contact with the spectre, so he walked out of the park, crossed the dual carriageway toward the mainline railway station. He had to get to London somehow. Find out what happened to his job.

The train station was likely to be busy at this time of night, people still heading out to Christmas Eve parties or coming home from daytime drinking sessions, or from days at work with employers who insisted on maintaining a skeleton staff.

Crosby felt skeletal himself, his paunch gone, obviously through lack of intake rather than excessive exercise. And his fingers bore the brown tarnish of regular tobacco usage, no doubt roll-ups scrounged from passers-by, or butts with a few drags left in them pilfered from street bins or foot flattened stubs peeled from pavements or scavenged from kerbsides.

He didn't like the attention his appearance attracted at the station, members of security staff and members of the public alike eyeing him with a mixture of disdain and intense disdain. The public house at the bottom of the ramp near the station car park looked tempting and had indeed tempted him to sample its wares many times in the past. On this night of nights, a surprisingly mild one for the time of year, both inn and beer garden were filled to overflowing like a frothing pint glass with the young warming up for a trip to a club uptown, just as he had done thirty years previously.

"Ghost? Ghost?" He detoured away from the pub to the parade of shops on the other side of the station, looking for the face of his spirit guide in the poles of streetlights, the posters of bus stops, the bark of trees, the glass of shut up or shut down shop windows. Why had he trusted an apparition and let him transport him to this mess of a world? A world in which his life was in an even more shoddy state than the one he'd inhabited previously?

At least in that miserable world he had a roof over his head and a bed under his bottom, even if he had no job. Here, he was sans everything, home, hope and employment. Devoid of purpose, even more so than in the world he'd been so eager to leave behind.

Walking the streets whispering for a ghost to help you on Christmas Eve? Come on. What a state your life has to be in for you to be doing that.

He turned back and walked onto the station concourse, seeing a security guy side-eyeing him and whispering sweet somethings into his walkie talkie. But even that wasn't the most newsworthy event happening at that moment, because there and then Crosby saw a familiar figure enter the stationers where, who knows how long ago, he'd dropped off Kyle to buy him and Marie their first ever Christmas presents. And there was Kyle in there again now, a different, harsher, harder Kyle who slipped a bar of Galaxy chocolate into his pocket, and a set of pink pens into a magazine about sewing which he rolled up and slipped under his jacket before calmly walking out of the shop.

Watching his son commit theft was something Crosby never thought he'd ever have to endure. But it had just happened right in front of him and there was nothing he could do or wanted to do about it.

"Travelcard?"

A guy in his fifties tapped Crosby on the shoulder and handed him an orange ticket.

"I've finished with it, mate. You look like you need it. Nice hat by the way."

Crosby stared at the ticket, its orange turning to gold in his hands. He nodded his thanks and slotted it into the thin of the ticket barrier's mouth, yanking it out on the other side and running down the ramp to Platform 4 to wait for a train that had a track record of being late it was eager to maintain.

Wandering along the aisle of the carriage fifteen minutes later, Crosby was conscious of wary looks from fellow passengers, each hoping he didn't choose the vacant seat next to them to park his behind.

Nose blind to his own stench, Crosby sensed he was leaving a far from pleasant odour in his wake, and settled for standing near the toilet, from which disturbing odours were regularly emanating.

As other passengers passed and turned up their noses at the smell, Crosby wafted his hand in front of his nose and pointed at the toilet door, happy for the steady stream of passengers who used the facility to take the blame for his unkempt state.

The journey into London Bridge only took twenty minutes, and Crosby was glad to be free from the confines of the train carriage and spread his scent on the platform as passengers filed toward the exit.

He chose to walk to The Anchor public house rather than risk a bus or underground train, neither of which had toilet facilities which he could blame for his smell.

The streets were loud with the drunk and getting drunk, work colleagues who'd been out since lunchtime knowing they ought to be heading home but thinking that this special day gave them the excuse to stay for just one more.

As he approached The Anchor, he could hear Terry's foghorn of a voice, followed by Tamsin's distinctive laugh. He was surprised to see them both arm in arm outside, surrounded by ten to twelve colleagues, only one or two of whom he recognised. He paused outside the pub until Terry caught his eye.

"What do you want, mate?" Terry asked, smiling but clearly drunk.

"Terry, isn't it?"

Terry's smile disappeared, his eyes narrowed, trying to place the face.

"How do I know you?" he asked.

"I'm Nick. We used to work together."

Terry's lower lip protruded, a grimace visiting his face before his whole head shook.

"I was a developer at Solarvecchi Zotte AI," said Crosby.

"Mate, there's been hundreds through the doors over the last few years."

Crosby was conscious of Tamsin staring at him. He smiled at her, an exchange Terry didn't appreciate.

"What you smiling at her for?"

"Tamsin, isn't it?" Crosby asked.

Tamsin instinctively withdrew behind Terry, using him as a barrier between herself and this man who claimed to know her.

Terry stepped forward. "Listen, mate, great to see you again and all that, but it's time to move along. I'm not in the mood for reunions with tramps like you."

"I just thought I'd say hello."

"Well, mission accomplished, now do one."

"I just wanted to know if you remembered what happened, to me, why I lost my job."

"I've already told you, we have hundreds of developers." Terry pointed across the street to the upper floors of an impressive twelve storey building constructed purely from glass it seemed, a white neon sign at its summit, bearing the legend, Solarvecchi Zotte AI. "How do you expect me to know?"

"Wow," Crosby exhaled. "Business must be good."

"Yeah, it is."

"How about one for the road, as it's Christmas."

Terry stepped forward for a nose to nose with Crosby. Tamsin tried to haul him back but missed his arm.

"It's him, Tez," Tamsin said. "He's the one who tried it on with me a few years back."

"That Nick?" Terry's tone changed from drunk happy to drunk aggressive in an instant.

She nodded.

"Now, I remember who you are," said Terry.

At least someone remembered something, Crosby thought.

The force of Terry's advance forced Crosby to back off into the street. "Calm down, Terry Christmas." Crosby smiled and shot him the middle finger like they always used to. Next he knew, a flash of pain struck his jaw and it was lights out on Christmas Eve. Crosby recalled hearing Tamsin scream before his head hit the pavement and the world blacked out.

Crosby had no idea how long he was dead to the world, but it was three minutes and a few seconds before he came round, sober passers-by bending the knee to tend to him.

His head felt fit to split, his thick hat cushioning some of his fall but not enough to stop the blood.

Crosby sat up and quickly regained his focus, wondering what the fuss was all about, pushing away those who were trying to help him, embarrassed at being the centre of attention.

He staggered off down the street, regularly inspecting the tender rear of his head. He walked he knew not where, because no direction could take him home when he had no home, every direction threatened danger, disappointment, even death.

"I want to go back," Crosby called out to the ghost. "How do I get back?"

Crosby stopped when he saw a rabbit hutch in a front garden, brand new sandy coloured wood and likely to be someone's present the following morning. They could live without the bag of hay inside he thought, removing it from the hutch. Make for a great pillow to get him some sleep.

He stumbled along the street, the lights of central London to his left, his head throbbing, his back aching, his feet reporting myriad sores. He stopped at what looked like an empty lot that had once housed a property but now contained overgrown grass along with signs promising redevelopment.

He stole through a gap in the wooden fence and set the hay down right by the fence in a spot the streetlights couldn't reach.

"What are you going to do if you go back?"

The voice of the ghost almost caused Crosby to choke on his own saliva.

"You've got to stop doing that," he moaned, seeing the ghost's likeness in the grain of the fence's wood.

"You want to go back to where you were before you came here, unemployed, miserable, and wondering if your life is worth it?"

"I'm doing exactly the same thing here, only there I could do it in a warm bed. I've got nothing here, no wife, no son, no job, no house."

"But you had those things before and you were miserable. Bemoaning your bad luck. Wanting to end it."

"Grass isn't always greener, huh?"

"There's no point keeping asking to go back. When you're going through hell, you have got to keep going."

Crosby shrugged.

"The deal was three, remember?"

"Ah yes, the small print I never got to read."

"Would you have read it if I'd showed you it?"

"Of course not, who do you think I am?"

"Aren't you the guy who helped develop tech that summarised copy in seconds, including small print?"

Crosby said nothing.

"Want to know how many people lost their livelihoods as a result of that technology?"

Crosby rolled away to face the fence.

"You've got to face what you've done sometime, Nicholas."

"I just need to rest," he said. "Let me rest."

# Chapter 5:
## Crosby's Second Rude Awakening

It is fair to say that second time around, Crosby was a little less surprised to wake and find himself in a different location to the one in which he'd fallen asleep. While to say he was getting the hang of things in terms of his ghost's ghostly ways would have been an exaggeration, Crosby was, however, beginning to accept the strange unpredictable nature of the events befalling him.

Having recalled falling asleep using a bundle of hay he'd borrowed from a seemingly deserted rabbit hutch as a pillow, he sat up a little too fast for his body's liking, the weight of his brain forcing him back down to the lateral. His head had been on a cushion, the rest of him on a black leather sofa that matched the one in his house. He recalled the punch from Terry Christmas that had floored him, causing him to hit his head on the pavement. His head still ached but the dried blood he expected to find at the back where contact was made with concrete wasn't there. To make up for it, his stomach churned, his pores sweated and his mouth bore the dryness of a man who'd traversed the desert for a day without drink.

Unless he was very much mistaken, which he wasn't, Crosby was sporting a momentous hangover. Early stages most likely, given the giddiness he still experienced and the darkness of the room. But he could see enough of his surroundings to know he was in his own living room, the Christmas decorations as he'd left them that morning, the tree lights on, room underneath for more presents than the lonely and only two currently in place.

Getting up to find out who they were for and from remained too much of a mission for Crosby, but he smiled to himself having escaped the horrors of homelessness, the panic of wandering the streets with nowhere to go, and the aftermath of being floored by a punch from a former colleague.

The ghost let me come back after one turn, he smiled to himself. Thanks, man.

After ten minutes of unsuccessfully trying to sleep off his headache-driven hangover, Crosby sat upright on the sofa and looked over to the window, the silhouette of a head and shoulders in the glass.

"Go away," he shouted, staggering over to the window and grumpily drawing the curtains.

He turned away. Wait a minute, Crosby thought on his way back to the sofa.

He quickly returned to the window, pulled open the curtains and peered out into the street. Whoever had been looking in was now ambling off toward the town centre.

Was that him, was that me? Crosby thought, recalling doing exactly the same thing in his previous reality.

He recalled walking like that down the street, but then this was his house and he'd walked down that street to get to the station to take him on the train to work a thousand times and more before. How could that person wandering off be him, when he was him, right here?

He closed the curtains on that conundrum more considerately this time, and turned to appreciate the cosy Christmessiness of the room.

The decorations made the space feel a little more claustrophobic than normal, but he liked how Christmas distinguished itself from other times of the year. It was something different, and different had to be cherished in a world that could deliver so much sameiness.

He stooped to pick up the two presents under the tree and checked the labels: To Mum from Kyle, To Dad from Kyle. It was the first time Kyle had bought and wrapped a gift for them and that meant something. Meant a lot actually. And not just a sure sign of his son maturing.

Crosby smiled to himself, recalling the first time he bought his parents a Christmas present – a carriage clock. He had no idea that was the sort of thing you bought someone as a retirement present rather than for Christmas, but they didn't let on. It felt so good to be able to surprise them with a gift.

He sat back down and checked his pulse, something he did regularly since his mental breakdown earlier in the year. A reassuring habit, not that it would be reassuring if the pulse he detected was too slow, too fast, or worse still, irregular.

Satisfied he was operating at normal beats per minute on this most abnormal night of the year, Crosby's attention turned to thinking about the ghost. He quickly concluded that the ghost was gone and Christmas was back to normal. The ghost had granted him his wish, like the genie in the bottle, and the weirdness of groundhog day was over. No three scenarios as threatened. Crosby was one and done.

He actually felt a bit short-changed even though he'd got his wish to return home.

But hold on. Why the headache? In his original reality, he'd lost his job earlier that day and gone straight home, despite the strong desire for a drinking session with Terry and the rest of them. Was the pain a hangover from the last reality when his head hit the pavement?

Crosby checked and confirmed he was still dressed in his work clothes. No sign of tent dwelling.

He checked his face. No beard either, just a day's growth of stubble that he'd shave in the morning as Marie didn't like anything but smooth.

For the first time, he became aware of his phone vibrating on the floor by the sofa. Perhaps this would prove to be the best way for him to piece together how he'd come to be here.

He was shocked to find 74 unread messages on his phone, many from Tamsin.

There were pictures too. Selfies of him kissing Terry Christmas outside the Anchor pub. Some of him kissing Tamsin outside the same pub. Her sitting on his lap inside the pub, smiling at him, short skirt, long black hair, all taken earlier that evening.

In a panic he deleted all the messages about and from her and all pictures of him and her.

Then he took a deep breath to prepare himself to confront his biggest fear. Had Marie checked his phone and seen those messages and pictures?

His blood thumped against the backs of his eyes. No need to check his pulse in his wrist or neck to know his heart was beating faster than normal.

Had he and Marie got to the checking each other's phone messages stage of their marriage? He certainly hadn't. His phone had been on the floor, could have fallen out of his pocket, or Marie could have taken it out and dropped it in disgust.

Crosby couldn't remember how he'd got back home. Oh, how complicated drinking makes life. Sobriety keeps things so simple, but so so dull.

He checked more of his message history – no mention of the job loss. From the evidence, Crosby had been sending messages all afternoon and well into the early evening. There was no mention of the restaurant table he'd booked for him and his family. That led him to experience another terrible feeling that he'd stayed in the pub with his workmates and got drunk all afternoon, rather than carry on a Christmas tradition and have lunch with his family.

Terry Christmas Merry.

What's going on?

He wanted to wake Marie to gauge her mood, see what she knew, but his phone was saying 02:12am early Christmas morning. Who'd be happy about being woken at that time, even by Santa?

Crosby couldn't stop himself feeling awful which forced him to lie back down and contemplate his state.

His body temperature felt several degrees above the normal Celsius and Fahrenheit, yet another reason to bemoan the terrible and terribly unfair impact alcohol had on the older body. Systems that had once been able to imbibe copious amounts of the stuff without feeling like death when its effects began to wear off.

Terrified of what he'd done, and annoyed that he couldn't remember doing any of it, Crosby failed to settle on the sofa, haunted by thoughts and flashbacks, some of which entailed Tamsin looking hot and smiling at him and her buying him a drink and he her and then it got messy and cloudy, but the desire was there and it was such a thrill and it was clear she reciprocated so what was the harm, it was Christmas after all. Married man. You're a married man.

One thing was for sure, he was free of the hard skin and beard of his previous reality, all that a distant memory even though in this reality it had never happened, something that could easily get confusing if he thought about it too much, so he vowed not to think about it much at all. Concentrate on the here and now. That was the only way to get through the Christmesses the ghost was getting him into.

He paced the lounge, wondering if he dare risk slipping into bed next to Marie, cuddling up for something Christmassy. If she pushed him out of bed, he'd know he was in trouble, that she knew he was up to something, that she'd seen his phone. He couldn't risk that, that would ruin Christmas. If she knew what he'd done, surely she'd keep it to herself for Kyle's sake? Let them enjoy a normal family Christmas, then let fly with the accusations on Boxing Day, maybe even the day after, the first of Betwixtmas.

As with the last reality, Crosby would need to ask leading questions to piece together how he came to be where he was and in the state he was in. Trouble was, those who could provide the answers were both asleep.

He ventured over to the window, a short walk that was indeed a venture in his current state, his co-ordination virtually out of the window. He peeked through a gap in the curtain. No snow falling, just the glitter of street lights in puddles, a few hunched shadows of people walking home to be together.

There were messages on his phone from Marie, sent at 1PM and 1:30 and 2:30. Where are you? We're outside the restaurant, where ought we to be?

2.54: This is a disgrace, Nick. We've come all this way and you have to work late on Christmas Eve? I'm coming to your office to urinate on your boss' desk.

Crosby had no idea how he'd prevented that messy situation from happening. Had he prevented it? Surely he'd remember. The knuckles on his right hand looked red, but he couldn't feel much. He seemed to remember Terry getting aggressive, saying they should go back into the office and destroy the place, kill the top brass, and take over the business for themselves, but surely that hadn't happened.

Or had it?

He remembered Terry talking to two guys with leaflets. Were they Luddites?

In the previous reality, AI had a skyscraping HQ with neon atop and Terry Christmas in charge. What about now? Sounded like he and Terry were still employed in the same middle management roles he had been on the day he was fired. Only this time, no firing.

There were no more messages from Marie until 5PM when she typed that she presumed he was on the train home. From the looks of the pictures on his phone from around that time, he was sitting on Tamsin's lap. In the pub.

His skin burned as his blood dropped a few more degrees in temperature.

He turned on the TV, flicking the volume down to zero.

In what seemed only a few seconds later, Crosby was awoken by a tap on his foot and was surprised to find himself in the same room he'd fallen asleep in.

"Merry Christmas, Dad."

Crosby's hangover was now full blown, evidenced by the aggro behind his eyes and the dislocation he felt when he sat upright. He squinted at the Christmas tree and saw it still only had two presents under it.

"I didn't realise Santa stopped visiting the moment you stopped believing in him," said Kyle glumly, and he left the room choking back tears.

Several expletives later, having checked his phone to see more messages from Terry and Tamsin and a time of seven oh five, Crosby rushed up to his bedroom.

"Go back to bed, Kyle," he shouted. "We'll start the day over."

Marie had overslept too and after he'd shaken her awake, they both panic-hunted down the hidden presents, Crosby wheeling the bike out of the cupboard and carrying it down the stairs, Marie following him with an armful of wrapped gifts.

Crosby hid the bike behind the curtain as planned, just a few hours later than planned, while Marie arranged the gifts under the tree, tearful when she saw the two from Kyle.

Crosby was convinced the sweat he was dripping contained enough alcohol to get him drunk all over again if he were foolish enough to gather it in a glass and partake, but he dismissed that as weird thinking.

"Ready, Kyle," he called upstairs.

"Too late."

"Come on, babe," Marie pleaded. "We're sorry."

"Longest lie-in I've had on Christmas morning since before he was born," Crosby whispered to his wife.

She didn't answer. Didn't even look at him.

Kyle peered round the door, his appearance greeted by an over the top exclamation of *Merry Christmas* from both his parents, not quite in unison, but both united in their desire to make amends for this terrible start to the day.

"What were you doing sleeping down here?" Kyle asked his dad, a hint of a smile on his face when he saw the number of gifts stacked under the tree.

"I got back late from work. I didn't want to wake your Mum."

"What do you mean you didn't want to wake me?" she scowled. "You banged the door down saying you couldn't find your key."

Crosby grimaced and realised more leading questions were required for him to escape from this unscathed.

"You were working that late?" Kyle asked him.

"Quite late, but we went out for a drink afterwards, as it's Christmas."

"But you missed the meal."

"I know. I'm sorry, son. Nothing I could do. Things are a bit tricky at work at the moment. Why don't you open your presents?"

Crosby ignored his phone rumbling text messages as he watched his son open his three games and more gifts from Marie and their relatives. Kyle looked nervous when he handed his Mum and Dad their gifts, Crosby's being a football magazine, a packet of Maltesers and a set of biros.

"I thought you could use those for work," said Kyle. "You must need some."

"That's great, son. Thank you so much. I'll do the crossword in the magazine on the train while I'm stuffing my face with chocolate."

Crosby looked over at Marie and knew what Kyle had bought his mother before she did: a bar of Galaxy chocolate, a set of pink pens and a magazine about sewing. He looked at his son and wondered if he'd kept the cash they'd given him and stolen those presents.

Marie struggled to hide her disappointment, but Kyle didn't notice. Crosby did, but was too preoccupied with the brain overload he felt coming on.

After all the presents had been opened, an awkward pause followed and it took Crosby a while to realise why – the others were waiting for the traditional final gift. The showstopper.

Crosby's heart sank. Would it still be in the bedside cupboard? In a different reality, he'd unwrapped that present, thrown the paper under the bed and hooked the receipt around it in readiness to take it back to the shop.

He excused himself from the living room, every step he took up to the bedroom filled him with increasing dread. He checked the bedposts. All four were in position, no signs of life. No wood shavings on the floor. Did he have time and the paper and ribbon to rewrap the gift? He dived onto the bed and opened the bedside table cupboard, moved his diary and alarm clock out of the way and there it was, still wrapped in peach paper with a red ribbon. At least something had gone his way.

As he shaped to leave the room, he finally surrendered to the continuous messages that were rumbling his phone. Surely not this many people wanted to wish him a Merry Christmas.

He sat on the edge of the bed and saw 23 unread messages from Terry Christmas. He started with the most recent and got no further.

*Can't believe it man. I know you didn't mean it. But I just got back from the hospital, and that tramp you hit. He's DEAD.*

Such a grave message required several readings for Crosby to make sure he'd read the words in the right order. DEAD. That's how you spelt it.

He checked his fist again. The knuckles on his right hand were definitely more red than the left. His veins were pumping low grade ice around his body now, or at least that's what it felt like. If this was a wind-up, it was a pretty intricate one from Terry and completely out of order. Just because he had no one to spend Christmas with, didn't mean he ought to be ruining other people's Christmases with wild, murderous lies.

Crosby tried to remember the last time he'd punched anyone and couldn't even remember the first time. He could remember sucking up a punch while holidaying with mates in Norfolk. Their car had been followed by some locals who flashed them to pull over in a layby on a dual carriageway which the driver did, and Crosby, being in the passenger seat wound down the window to talk to these lads who were a few years older than they were. But the locals could tell from their accents that Crosby and his mates were from London, so he thought the situation was diffused, but just before they drove off, the bloke aimed a punch at Crosby which connected with his left cheek through the open window but caused no pain or adverse reaction at all.

Did Terry Christmas mean to say that Crosby had thrown a punch and killed a man? A man in his fifties fatally downing another human being with his bare fist? On Christmas Eve?

"Dad, why are you taking so long?" Kyle called up.

"Be down in a minute."

Crosby's sweaty fingers haphazardly tapped a reply to Terry asking what he was on about and didn't he know it was Christmas Day?

Crosby pocketed his phone hoping never to receive a text message ever again from anyone, and grabbed his wife's gift and presented it to her downstairs along with a kiss to her scalp.

Her smile was strained as she tore off the wrap and opened the box to reveal the watch she'd wanted.

She smiled and shaped to close the box.

"You not going to put it on, Mum?" Kyle asked.

"Later."

She smiled weakly at Kyle and didn't look at or thank Crosby at all. That's when he knew she'd seen the messages on his phone from last night.

That phone had rumbled twice more during the great unwrapping of the under-appreciated watch, and Crosby made his excuses to go and check them out, but stopped before he left the room, realising that Marie must be thinking he was fielding messages from Tamsin.

It was no good. He had to read Terry's reply so went out into the kitchen, calling out as he walked did anyone want tea?

Kyle was a taker but Marie said no curtly.

He pulled out his phone.

*You connected with a good one. He went straight down. Banged his head on the pavement. We thought he was out cold. But it was worse than that. Much worse.*

Crosby rinsed his sore knuckles under the cold tap, like that would destroy the evidence that his fist had connected with someone and killed them. He looked around the kitchen for the ghost he needed to save him again. No sign of a face in the tea towels hanging from the oven handle, or in the knife rack missing one its knives, or the plate stack or bread bin or toaster.

Then a knock at the door.

"Who's that?" he called out in disgust, as if knocking on someone's door on Christmas Day were a crime.

Crosby heard Kyle's feet thump across the floor on his way to answer it, echoing the heavy beat of his heart, Marie just sitting in the chair staring at the Christmas tree, her watch still in its box by her feet.

To say Crosby's heart skipped a beat when an officer of the local constabulary filled the frame of the kitchen door is an understatement. It missed several beats and his blood pressure shot up while his knuckles burned like never before.

"Are you Mr Nicholas Crosby?"

There was no point him denying that. And things got rapidly less Christmassy from then on.

After the formalities were attended to, Crosby was allowed to dress in something that wasn't his work clothes before being guided out of the house and into the back of an awaiting police car. As this is not a police procedural story, you'll be spared the details, suffice to say that around about the time the turkey should have been browning in the oven nicely, Crosby found himself in a flat grey police cell, on a flat, six-foot-long surface that someone had the cheek to call a bed.

"You want to go back to living in a tent?"

Crosby shot up in shock, recognising the voice of the ghost, and seeing his face in the thickly painted grey cell door.

"Where've you been? Why did you let it get to this?"

"I'm your ghost. Not your keeper."

"This is awful. Worse than a tent. You've got to get me out of here."

"So you kept your job, and celebrated that good news by getting drunk with your workmates, getting frisky with a workmate, nearly getting into a fight with a workmate, and then actually punching a stranger who hit their head on the pavement and died?"

"Is that what happened? I can't remember any of it."

"Oh, you were sounding off like a good 'un. Proud of the money you were making, the promotion you'd been given, the job stealing AI you'd been developing. There were plenty in that pub wanting to swing for you. But it took a passing homeless man who called you a job murderer for the violence to erupt."

"I still don't remember."

"And to make matters worse, you were out drinking with workmates when you were meant to be lunching with your wife and son."

"Yes, yes. OK. I'm a bad person. I've had a bad year. I fancied a drink."

"You're getting your realities in a twist, Nick. You haven't had a bad year at all. You got promoted for making Solarvecchi Zotte AI a fortune by developing tech that's made millions of people jobless. Feels good does it?"

Crosby lay back on the flat surface. "I don't know what's going on," he said. "But it seems like I can't win. I either lose my job and face ruin, or I keep my job, get a promotion, but cause someone to lose their life. And in both scenarios, I'm responsible for loads of people losing their livelihoods."

"Like I said before, I don't control what happens. You do. No one forced you to go out drinking yesterday to celebrate getting promoted. And no one forced you to take a regular salary doing a job that costs other people their jobs."

"It's Christmas. Everyone's entitled to let their hair down."

"And people are entitled not to have their jobs stolen by machines. And your wife and son are entitled to eat a meal they'd travelled up to London to enjoy with you. And a homeless man is entitled to share his opinion without losing his life."

Every mention of actions Crosby couldn't remember carrying out hurt nearly as much as the retina straining light in the cell.

"Understood. Understood." Crosby leaned toward the door. "Look, you said I get to experience three scenarios. I'm ready for the third, I need to see the third. Right now."

"What if your fate is worse than this?"

"How could anything be worse than this?"

"True, it's not very festive in here. It's like a bedroom in that sense."

Crosby stared at the apparition, wondering again how he knew that's what Crosby thought about bedrooms at Christmas.

"Remember, I only transport you between the realities. I'm not responsible for what happens once you get there."

"I know, I know. Just get me there, please."

"Usually the third is the best choice, the pick of the bunch, the cream of the crop. But I've never seen a one and two as grim as yours, so three has got to be an appealing option for you."

"I hope so. To be honest, I'll take anything over this."

"Reckon you can sleep under this light?"

"I can do it. I have to do it."

"We can't force these things, you know."

"I need to get out of here."

"Quite. You'll be convicted of manslaughter if you stay, I suspect, so won't be an official murderer, not that anyone can really tell the difference outside of the legal profession. You killed a man. That'll make it tricky for you to find work after your sentence which could be, who knows how long?"

"You're not making it any easier for me to sleep."

"No, you're right, sorry."

The ghost withdrew into the grey door so that the outline of his face was barely visible. Crosby's eyelids flickered, a tell tale sign of sleep being hard to find.

He took three deep breaths in a row, turned on his side to face the wall away from the glare of the retina thrashing light. More deep breaths. Sheep. Equations. Recipes. Counting backwards from one thousand. Christmas cracker jokes… Bingo.

# Chapter 6:
## The Final, Most Christmessy Reality

Crosby woke with a start and felt whatever he was sitting on rotate beneath him. He stretched out an arm and found a flat wooden surface in front of his face he used to steady himself. His eyes flicked open and explored his surroundings. Daylight. An open laptop in front of him in an office. Nothing else on the desk, the rest of the room tidy. A line of photos on the wall of himself shaking hands with various B-list celebrities – soap actors, broadcasters, reality TV show contestants. Above these, pride of place, in a frame larger than the others even though the photo was smaller, a photo of Crosby shaking hands with the King, a meeting he had zero recollection of.

In the bookcases to his left and right, a distinct lack of books, although some technology magazines bookended jagged glass and cheap metal awards from various small-time sector specific ceremonies. Best Use of AI. Most Innovative Machine Learning. Automation of the Year. If they were his, he couldn't recall winning them.

Behind him, a window. He stood up, immediately conscious of something not being right, the weight around his midriff hefty. He tapped a fulsome belly with his right hand, then explored buttons of a white shirt that were straining to restrain his bulging gut that overhung his belt.

He shuffled to the window and scissored a bigger gap in the beige Venetian blinds with his thumb and forefinger, and looked out over High Holborn, Christmas displays in the windows of the stores on the opposite side of a street busy with buses and taxis and cyclists and pedestrians crossing, bright colourful lights arching across the road from upper window to upper window, lampposts wrapped with tinsel and lights forming static stars, angels, snowflakes and bells.

Back in his office, he explored the cabinets, discovering three limited edition bottles of Jack Daniel's in one, the thought of drinking causing him to realise that he had no headache. Was that a problem? Potentially. How could not having a headache be a headache?

Crosby fumbled in the pockets of the jacket his chair was wearing for his phone. Pulled out a diamond studded case, housing a fairly ordinary handset by comparison – glittering gold. Habituated now to the need to find out as much information as he could about his new reality as quickly as he could, his phone revealed some vital statistics: Same day and same year as the previous reality. But an earlier start. Just gone noon, Christmas Eve. No other messages and a contacts page thin on contacts.

Where were all the names of friends, family? He scrolled. No Kyle. No Marie.

He woke his laptop from its slumber, needing it to provide more clues, his attention immediately drawn to two files on the desktop. He opened the one labelled 'Latest Iteration'. Scanning the code within, he knew this. He knew the power of what it represented to replicate the brilliance of the work coders like he and Terry were doing.

He closed the file and clicked open the folder below it labelled 'Redundancies'. Only one file within – a draft of an email and a list of the names of seven employees.

Crosby read the email. Word for word it was the same message he'd read himself in the alternate reality in which he'd lost his job. Now his tension peaked for another reason. He opened his email app, heading straight to the sent folder. And there it was. Sent to multiple recipients. The message to the severed seven. Firing them on the spot on Christmas Eve. Sent by him to them, literally twenty minutes ago.

He had no recollection of clicking send, of course. Why couldn't he have been transitioned here twenty minutes earlier? There's no way he would have sent that message and put those people through the agony of unemployment. And how had he found the arrogance to take a power nap after sending such a destructive message?

He scrambled forlornly to see if there was any way to retrieve the message, knowing it was too late, the damage done, the cold words already sent and read and reacted to.

Crosby stood and paced the office, knowing what the employees outside were going through.

He edged open the door, saw the backs of three security guards blocking the entrance to the corridor that led from the top brass offices where he was, to the main open plan section. There were three more offices, the CTO's opposite to the left, the CFO opposite to the right and the COO next door. He quickly checked them all, finding them all locked and empty. The only other room was the C-suite ensuite, the toilet reserved for top brass arse, with bidet, shower and always fresh towels.

Crosby knew he had to bide his time. Wait for Terry Christmas and the others to be escorted out of the building by security as the email message directed. No point going out among the people and trying to reason with them after sacking them. Let them go down the pub and get drunk and while they were down there make a quick exit and stay away from the office until new year when things should have calmed down, the rage blown over.

He returned to his desk, pulled open the top drawer, discovering three unwrapped cigars and car keys with a Maserati fob and some kind of device he presumed gave him access to the underground car park restricted for the use of senior management like himself. But of more interest was the notepad he found with a scribble on the top sheet.

*Tammy. 1PM.*

With what he'd experienced, it didn't take a genius to work out what was going on. Crosby was disgusted with himself. Tamsin was one of the best coders and deserved better than to be dragged into his mess of a world. What did she see in him anyway, his gut, his indeterminate jaw line? Can't have been the money, she was on one of the best salaries in the business, as befitted her talent.

He looked around for any other clues that would give him an insight into his situation. Checked his inbox and outbox, both of which were low on content, like they'd been cleaned out as recently as this morning. The only sent messages were those announcing the redundancies.

His internet history revealed a fascination with all things AI, visits to sites about streamlining the payroll, sites offering tickets to online conferences, URLs focusing on automating processes. All so dull and diligent. So this is what you had to do to make CEO.

His desktop phone lit red. Not having seen such a contraption for years let alone used one, he pressed the red light discovering it did nothing, so he lifted the receiver.

"Hello?"

"Just checking to see you called your son back, Mr Crosby."

"I... er... yes, I did. Although he may call again."

"Shall I put him through when he does?"

"Of course."

"It's just that you don't normally..."

The person on the other end of the line, whom Crosby presumed was his secretary, faltered.

"I don't normally, what...?"

"You don't normally like taking non-work calls during office hours. Sir."

That sounded incredibly out of character for Crosby. But exactly the sort of thing you needed to do if you wanted to make CEO and stay CEO.

"Well, it's Christmas," he said, making light of it. "You'll be off home soon?"

Another pause. "Errr... you asked me to stay all day, sir. Until six in fact. A bit of unpaid overtime."

Crosby shook his head. "Nonsense. Sorry. You take the rest of the day off..." He paused, unsure if it was Katie on reception he was speaking to, or the CEO's PA whom he never spoke to and didn't know the name of. "Go home, or down the pub and have a great Christmas," he added.

"Thank... thank you sir."

Crosby could tell what he was saying was massively out of character for the role into which he'd transitioned.

He heard shouting from the open plan office area. Knew it would be Terry Christmas kicking off. Best let him get on with it, although Crosby had to admit that he was dying to see who was sitting next to Terry in his chair at his desk. What if his current version of Crosby saw that version of Crosby? That could ruin the whole parallel universe time continuum thing. Not something he could risk. Don't mess with stuff you don't understand. Stay where you are, he told himself. And so he did.

He checked his watch. Gone half twelve.

He needed to call his son. He scrolled his contacts on his phone again. Still no Marie or Kyle of course, although there was a 'K' contact. He navigated to recent calls. K appeared only once or twice in the list. Had to be him. Tamsin's name appeared far more frequently but he needed to gloss over that for now.

As Crosby was about to dial K, a knock at the door.

"Come in."

One of the security guards poked his head in.

"A Miss Adams to see you, sir."

Crosby was disgusted at the pulse of electricity that announcement generated in him.

"Send her in," he said sternly, covering his excitement with a placid and measured tone of voice.

Crosby adjusted his tie, tried to flatten his paunch and sat as casually as he could in his office chair. He enjoyed the comfort of the leather seat, the smooth rocking motion and turning arc preferable to the hard and static chairs out there in the open plan area.

Tamsin walked in without knocking, looking stunning in a black shirt and skirt, lipstick thickly painted across her mouth, eyes encircled by mascara, smelling like, well, the cliché would be a million dollars, although being a proud Brit, Crosby would always prefer that to be expressed in sterling.

"How's things out there?" he asked, motioning to her to shut the door and take a seat.

"Terry's kicking off as you'd expect. Joel's giving it some too."

Joel, Crosby thought to himself. Not a name he recognised. Must be the person in what was his role.

Tamsin eyed Crosby seductively, like she was expecting him to make a move. But this hardly seemed the right time and place. And if he was being honest with himself, which he was about to be, his sex drive was at an all time low, knowing the kind of Christmas he'd just inflicted upon half of his employees with the email he'd sent, many of whom were colleagues in a different reality.

"You not going down the pub?" Crosby asked Tamsin.

"Of course, but I thought you wanted to..."

She hitched her skirt north a seductive inch and eyed the desk. Crosby despaired at the body and mind he'd inherited.

"I'm taking my wife and son out to lunch," he said, watching her closely to gauge her reaction. The use of the term wife almost caused Tamsin to fall off her chair.

"Wife?"

"Ex-wife, I mean."

That didn't have the desired effect either. "You said she was dead."

"Oh. She is. I'm taking my son to see her grave."

"With your lunch?"

"Yes, we have a sort of Christmas lunch over her grave. It's a family tradition."

Tamsin grimaced, as if she were seeing Crosby in a different light. A more macabre light.

"That's sick."

"It's an acquired taste, for sure."

"So, I got dressed up for nothing?"

"I might make it down the pub later. Anchor is it?"

"Isn't it always? You're on a weird one today. Couldn't take your eyes off me earlier. Now this."

She stood up and headed for the door.

"You're looking great, Tamsin."

She paused but didn't look round and continued to walk out.

"Oh, one more thing before you go."

She stopped and turned to face him.

"How you are getting on with your job?"

From her reaction this was an unexpected ask.

"I mean, the ethical side of things. Are you OK with that?"

Tamsin removed the gum from her mouth. "Not breaking any laws doing what we're doing, are we."

"Well, no, but that's because there are no laws. We're self-governing to a large degree."

"Yeah. I never think too much about the impact beyond these four walls. I like the job, I like the money, I like the people most times when they're not acting weird. I'm sorry about people losing their jobs to machines, but that's progress, I guess. We're thinking AI can create a whole load of new job opportunities, aren't we?"

Crosby smiled weakly, doubting very much that was the case. He nodded. "OK, as long as you're OK about being one of the surviving three?"

She shrugged. "Job losses are inevitable, right?"

Crosby forced an even weaker smile. "Hopefully I'll see you down the pub later."

"Enjoy your graveside lunch, sicko" she said, and was gone.

Crosby walked over and shut the door and inhaled that million dollar smell Tamsin left in her wake. He returned to his laptop, searched the exchange rate. A million dollars came in at £788,180 today. Still an impressive amount to smell. Terry would be impressed by that. In a different reality.

He tapped his phone and pressed it to his ear.

"Kyle? Oh, great, it is you. It's Dad.... Yeah, Dad. Father, yes Father. My secretary said you called… for sure we're still meeting. A tradition is a tradition, right? I booked it for, two I think. O'clock. Yeah, two people for two o'clock. But get here anytime… OK, meeting outside the restaurant is fine. La Spatchas, down by the station. You know how to get there. See you there."

Kyle had sounded miserable. Crosby suddenly wondered how his son was getting there. If his mother wasn't around, that was some journey for a twelve-year-old to be making alone. He checked his phone contacts again. Definitely no Marie.

In a panic, he redialled and waited. But Kyle didn't answer, and Crosby didn't wait for the answerphone announcement.

With Kyle sorted, sort of, Crosby next needed to know about Marie. What had happened to her? Had they fallen out, divorced? Had she died? If so, how had she died? Not the sort of questions a father could ask a son over lunch.

*Kyle, pass me the salt and tell me how your mother died, I've forgotten.*

Said son would expect said father to know the answer to life critical questions such as was his wife dead? Even if it was likely she was his ex-wife at the time.

Crosby filled the intervening time before he was due to meet Kyle listening for any trouble coming from the open plan area of the office, and playing Solitaire on his computer. There are things you've got to do when you're CEO, he imagined. It can't all be work, else you'd explode from overwork.

At ten-to-two he shouldered his jacket, pocketed his keys and cigars and edged toward the door to the office. He slowly opened it, pausing the movement at the first sign of a creak. The trio of security guards had gone. Pulling the door further open, he crept out into the carpeted corridor and slowly walked toward the reception area which lay between his office and the open plan office.

The receptionist had gone home. So had everyone else. Home or the pub. Crosby suspected that in different circumstances he would have been enraged by the lack of skeleton staff minding the fort. But he didn't want to see people now. He wanted to get out.

He took the lift just in case something was happening on the stairs. Emerged at ground level to hear that Leni's tip for the 1.40 hadn't come in.

"Bloody sixteen to one shot won it. Carechi's something. Still, I got a tip for the 2.10." For a moment, Crosby considered it, but refused the advice based on previous performance.

"Are you on it?" he asked Leni.

"Just a cheeky twenty."

"Merry Christmas, Leni, hope it comes in for you."

Leni looked takenaback when Crosby offered his hand and stood for the shake.

"Merry Christmas to you, sir."

Leni sniffed extra hard, trying to spy alcohol on Crosby's breath.

Crosby let himself out and felt uncomfortable in his shiny shoes as he faced the hustle and, yes, the bustle of main street London on Christmas Eve.

The weather had held grey and stayed mild for the time of year, though the wind ruffled a few feather boas of those who were off to glamorous parties in posh hotels.

Why had Crosby booked mid-range La Spatchas to the east when he could have afforded to follow the majority of the human traffic west in the opposite direction to the classier, more expensive eateries?

A tradition was a tradition.

The route to La Spatchas was paved with the homeless, squatting by walls and sheltering in the doorways of shut down businesses. A printer's gone bust. A book shop gone to the wall, the half-ripped closing down sale must end, everything must go poster still taped to the window. He turned on the spot to admire the building from which he'd just emerged. Taller by a few floors than he'd ever seen it, the neon red and white, spelling out Solarvecchi Zotte AI a word at a time like a casino on the Vegas strip.

All Crosby could think about was the size of his bank balance as he strode past the poor who were quietly screaming for pennies. Holding out polystyrene cups and card readers, hoping to magnetically attract coins or plastic to save their day, their Christmas, their life. Crosby would have stopped at a cashpoint to check his account if he knew the PIN.

As he reached La Spatchas, he saw Kyle walking toward him, hair neatly combed, looking every inch the perfect son. Crosby noted Kyle withdrew his hands from his pockets the moment he saw his father. He sported a pristine white shirt – a first for outside school – and smart black trousers plus grey jacket. All that was missing was the bow tie and his son could have been dressed to serve tables at La Spatchas rather than eat at one.

Crosby reached to hug his son, but Kyle pulled away, offering his hand for shaking instead.

"Bit formal. I like it," said Crosby, feeling awkward.

They shook and Crosby held the restaurant door open for Kyle, a wasted gesture as once inside, Crosby had to go first to confirm the reservation.

"We got you your favourite table," the waitress said, waiting for him to walk toward it.

A moment of panic. All the tables bar three were vacant, and Crosby had no clue where his favourite table was, and was even a little disgusted about the concept of having a favourite table being a thing.

"After you," Crosby genuflected in the direction of the girl.

He invited Kyle to follow her as she led them to a horseshoe shaped private booth a little way away from the other tables, but next to another private booth, currently empty.

As father and son got themselves comfortable sitting next to each other rather than opposite, Crosby stopped, noting the sign announcing the soups. Tomato, chicken and winter vegetable.

Brain ache followed which he planned to dismiss by ordering wine.

"What are you drinking, son?"

"Coke, please."

"I think we can do better than that."

Kyle looked at him.

"There comes a time, and it's usually Christmas time, when a boy has to get his first taste of what life's like being a man."

Crosby stopped, momentarily distracted by a vision of his son swigging from a bottle in Fairfield Park.

"You haven't tried alcohol yet?"

"Of course not."

"Good, because that's a moment that should be reserved for a father and son to share."

He picked a tame, tasty wine from the menu that retailed for close to three figures.

When the bottle arrived, Crosby poured a taster into Kyle's glass. They clinked and his son smiled and took his first sip, quickly followed by the second.

"Like it?"

Kyle shrugged and this time it was Crosby's turn to smile.

Both father and son selected winter vegetable as their soup, and other food that really isn't of interest. While they waited, Crosby tried to make conversation more successfully with his son than was the norm, which he put down to the effects of the wine.

"So what are your plans for Christmas?" Crosby asked him.

"I told you last week. I'm staying with Auntie Karla."

That must be Marie's sister, Crosby thought, trying to remember what she looked like.

"Where does she live?"

Kyle frowned. "Clapham, of course."

"Still? I thought they were moving," said Crosby, trying to cover for his lack of knowledge. "I'm sure they mentioned moving last time I... messaged them."

If Kyle was off celebrating with the maternal side of his family, what plans had he made for Christmas if they didn't involve his son or his wife? Same as last year? Which was?

"Didn't you go there last year?" he asked Kyle, who nodded. "Same as every year since Mum died."

Hmmm. There was the elephant in the room right there. An elephant only he could see. How did Marie die? He had to know. But his son would expect him to know, so he couldn't ask.

"It was so sad what happened, I'm sorry," Crosby said, examining Kyle's face closely for any reaction, hint of disdain, flicker of anger. Nothing.

The waitress arrived with their soups, accompanied by bread and individually wrapped rectangles of butter.

"Why don't you come to mine this Christmas?" Crosby announced after both had gone through the rigmarole of eating their soup by guiding the spoon away from their mouth in the bowl before drawing it into their mouth for the kill.

Kyle nearly choked on his last mouthful of winter vegetable, mopping his corners with his napkin.

Something about my house that makes that suggestion crazy? Crosby wondered, before wondering where his house was. Perhaps it wasn't a good idea to invite Kyle.

"I thought you didn't like Christmas?" said Kyle.

"When did I say that?"

"Every Christmas since Mum died."

"It's not the same without your mother around, that's for sure. That's probably why I don't like it."

"You were never home at Christmas when she was alive, always working. And too tired to enjoy Christmas Day."

"Sounds like I've got a lot to make up to you then, doesn't it?"

"Auntie Karla has arranged everything now, I can't cancel."

Crosby took another gulp of wine, the odds of a Christmas alone just massively increasing.

"Maybe next year."

Kyle nodded and drained his glass.

The rest of the meal passed by with small plates of expensive food being demolished mainly by Kyle, Crosby's appetite waning as the clock clicked closer to the time Kyle would leave him and then what? He didn't even know where he lived, what car he drove, actually, what car he couldn't now drive, thanks to the wine. A Maserati?

The meal continued with an accompaniment of small talk and a side order of awkwardness, Crosby filling his son's glass a little whenever the silences dragged on for more than ten seconds.

Despite the alcohol in his system, Kyle definitely wasn't in the running for throwing conversation topics into the ring. That responsibility fell to Crosby, who struggled for angles of interest, understandably when you consider the limited time he'd spent with his son.

"Do you go to Fairfield Park much?" he asked.

"What?"

It was an out of the blue question for sure with an ulterior motive behind the asking.

"I've heard there's a lot of homeless in there" said Crosby.

"There's homeless everywhere, Dad. That's why what you do is so embarrassing."

That took Crosby by surprise.

"You're embarrassed by my job?"

"I used to be proud to tell my mates you worked in AI. Now, it's just too dangerous to even mention it."

The wine was certainly loosening his son's tongue.

"What do you mean?"

"I got into a fight yesterday with someone at school whose mum and dad both lost their jobs recently."

Crosby felt something inside him sink, not just his heart, but all of his other vital organs too.

"What's that got to do with me?"

"Everyone knows what you do. Everyone suspects that the salaries of the people your tech is making redundant are going in your pocket. I wish I'd never mentioned it to anyone."

Kyle threw down his spoon and patted the corners of his mouth again with his napkin, looking out of the window, tears threatening to spill from his eyes.

"I don't develop job stealing tech," said Crosby.

Kyle shook his head. "I want to go home. Can I have it please?"

"You don't want dessert?"

"No, I'll just take whatever it is and go, thanks."

"Have I missed something?" Crosby asked.

"When we spoke earlier, you said you had something for me for Christmas?"

"Ah yes, of course. I knew there was something. I left them in the office. I'll have to go back. Come with me."

"What?"

"Just pop in and pick up the stuff. I'll call you a cab to Karla's."

Kyle shrugged. Sounded like a plan, better than the bus tube bus he'd have to catch otherwise.

Crosby called for the bill and settled up in cash, smiling at the waitress after she'd counted the twenties.

"Make sure you take that for yourself," he told her.

She seemed shocked more than surprised by his generosity.

"Merry Christmas," he added.

"Thank you, sir. I don't know what to say."

"Don't say anything."


The light was fading as father and son took the short walk back to Solarvecchi Zotte AI HQ. Crosby assumed that Terry and the rest of team he'd sacked plus the remaining three and a few from HR would be down The Anchor, located down Chancery Lane, a side road they crossed on their journey. As they walked, Crosby recognised a tramp stumbling toward them. He couldn't be sure, but his eyes and face took him back to that knuckle-reddening punch outside the pub.

"Where are you going?" Crosby asked the tramp, stepping in front of him.

"What's it to you?" the tramp growled.

Crosby took in a whiff of a musty, dank smell he recognised in himself.

"Quite a lot actually. But you wouldn't understand."

"I'm looking for money so I can get a roof over my head tonight and see Santa come down the chimney," said the tramp, making himself chuckle.

"How much do you need?"

The tramp laughed more heartily. "I'll take whatever I can get."

Crosby handed him fifty pounds in twenties and a ten. Kyle looked as amazed at the gesture as the recipient.

"Merry Christmas." The tramp smiled a toothless one and continued on his way, shaping to turn down Chancery Lane in the direction of The Anchor public house, outside of which Crosby knew a drunk and likely aggressive Terry would be drinking, along with a whole load of other bitter ex-Solarvecchi Zotte AI employees.

"Now where are you going?"

"Well, I figured after what you just gave me, it must be my lucky night. I'm off to see if anyone else is feeling as generous as you."

"They won't be. And I'll give you twenty more to walk that way."

He pointed west into the centre of town.

"Just been that way, governor. Busy up there," said the tramp shaking his head.

"Busy is good, right? More people like me ready to tip."

"More people like me looking for a tip."

"I'll give you another twenty and you can call it a night, surely?"

"You seem determined to be nice to me today. Why?"

"You look like a nice guy. I don't want to see you get hurt. Lots of drunks out today."

The tramp shrugged, took the money and walked back in the direction from which he'd just come, watched by Crosby until he reached the door of Solarvecchi Zotte AI HQ.

Leni signed Kyle in at reception, keeping things formal, still unsure what had happened to the normally surly Crosby who usually barely looked at him, let alone talked to him.

"Just give me five and I'll get your presents," Crosby said, letting himself and his son into the second floor office.

Crosby noted his son looking around like this was all new to him.

"You've never been in here before?"

Kyle shook his head. "You've never invited me."

"Have I not?" Crosby shook his head in disbelief at himself. What a piece of work.

He led his son into the office, with zero confidence he'd find a gift in there, having already explored the room.

"I'm sure I put it here," he said, sliding open the drawers of his desk not for the first time that day.

After ten minutes of fruitless searching, he pressed a few buttons on the desktop handset, knowing calling his secretary was pointless as he'd sent everyone home. "You do a nice thing like give your secretary the afternoon off, and it comes back to bite you on the arse," he said out loud, the frustration boiling over.

"Don't worry about it, Dad, it doesn't matter."

"It does matter."

He'd already checked every cupboard, every drawer. No signs of a gift. In desperation more than hope, Crosby opened the drinks cabinet and pulled out one of the bottles of Jack Daniel's.

"Ah yes, now this was one of yours," he said. "I just haven't had a chance to wrap it."

"I'm 12 years old, Dad."

"I know how old you are, son. I was there at your birth. I wanted you to have this bottle and save it until you're sixteen, seventeen. It'll be worth something then if you don't like the taste."

Kyle shook his head and Crosby reluctantly returned the bottle to the cupboard, recalling the drunken Kyle he'd met in Fairfield Park. Probably for the best that his son didn't start on the whiskey just yet. He'd likely be feeling tired from the wine right now anyway.

"Remind me what you wanted for Christmas, Kyle."

"Seriously, it doesn't matter. Don't worry about it."

"No, I do worry about it. I bought those presents. I just can't remember where I hid them."

"You can't remember where you hid a bike?"

"Oh, the bike!" Crosby had to think fast about the bike. "I've arranged for that to be delivered to your Aunt's," he lied. "It should be there now. If it isn't there when you get there, get Karla to call me and I'll chase them up. Bang a few heads together at the shipping company."

"Don't do that, Dad."

"I wouldn't really bang any heads together, son, it's just a figure of speech."

An awkward silence.

"I should go now," Kyle announced.

Crosby didn't like how relieved he felt to hear his son say that.

"I've enjoyed today," Crosby told him. "Good to catch up."

Kyle forced a smile.

"Did you enjoy your first experience of wine?"

"Actually, it was OK."

Crosby nodded.

"Yeah, your mum was a fan. I can take it or leave it. But as it's Christmas…"

He was unsure whether a kiss or a hug constituted their usual method of saying goodbye and settled on offering his hand which Kyle shook weakly.

"You need to work on your grip, son. A good grip shows you mean business."

"I'm not sure I do mean business, Dad."

As a disappointed Crosby walked his even more disappointed son to the lift, a crash rocked the building at street level, followed by shouting from downstairs. Crosby directed Kyle to head back into the office while he rushed over to the stairwell window. Down below in the wintry dusk of High Holborn, a mob of about twenty drunks blocked the road, all facing the Solarvecchi Zotte AI HQ, some kicking at the windows, others backing off into the street, causing cabs to swerve and buses to stall, while pedestrians on the far side of the road gawped and pointed.

Crosby ran back into reception, passing Kyle who followed his father into his office.

"What's happening, Dad?"

Crosby could tell from the pitch of his son's voice that he was scared.

"I need to go down and help," Crosby said.

"What?"

"You stay here, you'll be fine. Shut the door when I leave and don't open it until I get back."

"But…"

"Help yourself to anything. Except…"

Crosby slid open the drinks cabinet door and pulled out a different bottle of Jack, holding it by its neck, testing it for comfort, size and heft as a weapon. Its square shape and thick glass meant it passed and he rushed out of the office gripping it, descending a staircase he thought he'd descended for the last time earlier that day while being escorted from the building.

Reaching the first floor where HR plied their dubious trade, the shouting from the lobby continued, only louder, Leni's stern voice more distinct, him threatening to call the police, then announcing he was actually calling the police, and then a thud.

"You're not going up there," Leni insisted. "You've been fired. I know this. I've been told to watch out for you. Not let you back in."

"We're going up there whether you like it or not." That was Terry's voice and he sounded drunk and from the sounds of the feet and the cheering that followed his declaration, he'd returned to the office mobhanded.

"Try and stop us and you'll pay for it." That was someone else's voice.

Crosby cursed himself for letting the security guards off work early, especially when he saw one of them had returned as part of the mob intent on who knew what.

He ran upstairs back into the reception area, placing the bottle on the desk and slamming the entrance door, wedging a chair under its handles.

"Kyle," he called out.

He looked around for other items he could use to block the doorway, knowing it was all pointless with so many angry people down there, but anything to slow them down or give him fair warning of their approach.

"We need to go," he told his son in the calmest voice he could muster.

"I didn't want to come back here in the first place," said Kyle, on the verge of tears. "If you hadn't forgotten my presents, I'd be halfway home by now."

"I've still no idea where they are, I'm sorry, but we have more pressing problems right now."

"I'm scared, Dad."

"That's the wine talking. It's making you emotional. You should have stuck to water. Now just do what I say and follow what I do and we'll be out of here in no time."

He led Kyle through the open plan office area, past the desk that in another reality had been his, to the far end where the kitchen area led to emergency exit stairs down to street level.

Crosby pushed the door. Locked. He peered through the rectangular window, its glass reinforced with wires forming squares like the pages of a maths book.

He ran over to the kitchen sink and grabbed the kettle that stood bedside it. He returned to the door and beat the window with the kettle, but this glass was made strong and the appliance made no difference.

"What's the point of having an escape door that's locked?" Crosby asked the absent architects of the HQ.

Then he heard thumps at the entrance door across the other side of the office.

"We need to hide," he told Kyle.

"Are they after you, Dad?"

"They're friends of mine."

"It's because of your job, isn't it?"

"Crosby!" Terry shouted. "I know you're in here."

"He doesn't sound very happy."

"Get under there." Crosby pointed Kyle to Tamsin's desk, the underneath of which wasn't visible from the entrance. Crosby picked the desk next to it which benefited from a similar positioning.

Crosby could hear his son's heavy breathing and put his finger to his lips. Kyle took a deep breath and slipped in his EarPods, closed his eyes and imagined he was somewhere else.

"This is where the trappings of success get you," the ghost told Crosby, causing him to jump and bang his head on the underside of the desk he was under, its ghostly face warping the creases of the white bag in the wastepaper basket.

"Where have you been?" Crosby whispered, turning his mouth away from his son so Kyle couldn't see he was speaking.

"I've told you, you're not my only client."

"I'm in mortal danger here."

"I can see that."

"I thought you said this reality would be better, nicer."

"I said it ought to be. I didn't guarantee it would be."

"I'll be lucky to get out of here alive."

The banging on the outside of the door increased in volume as the voices increased in number.

"Just to satisfy my curiosity before whatever happens happens, what happened to Marie?" Crosby asked.

The ghost's face froze momentarily. "I don't know everything. Why don't you ask your son?"

Crosby glanced over at Kyle, clearly trying to distract himself with the music he was listening to.

"I can't ask him, can I? He'll expect me to know. You know what happened to her, don't you? Was it my fault? Was it down to me that my son has no mother?"

"You don't want to know."

"I definitely do now you've said that. I can't carry any more guilt around with me."

"Marie took her own life, Nick. All her work dried up. You told her she didn't need to work because you were making so much money, thinking that would make her happy. But art wasn't just a job to her. It was a passion she was lucky enough to get paid for. Until AI came along, that is. That's when the work dried up. Because your tech enabled people without a passion or talent for art to generate their own in seconds without hiring a genuinely talented artist like Marie. You put machines before humans, Nick. You devalued your wife's life's passion by inventing machines trained on work from genuine artists that churned out images. You took the joy and rarity out of art. What did you expect your wife to do, get down on her knees and thank you for destroying her career?"

Crosby slumped under the desk, looking over to his son, lost in a world of music, unwilling to face the inevitable.

"Isn't it inevitable that machines take over the Earth?" he asked. "I mean, if I don't invent this tech, someone else will, right?"

"Nothing is inevitable. And there's simply no need for anyone to develop tech that replaces artists and writers, or makes those with zero talent or passion think they can become an artist or writer without some kind of learning, skill or effort. There's no need at all for AI in the world of creativity. Why are developers like you even working in that area?"

"Because it's fun, and because…"

Crosby stopped himself.

"You were going to say because there's loads of money to be made, weren't you?"

The door to the creative floor separated from its hinges with a crash, and the sound of many footsteps and snorts announced the arrival of the mob.

Crosby turned to the wastebin but he knew the ghost would be gone before he saw the ghost was gone.

He listened to the invaders exploring the office, before the inevitability of discovery, Kyle first.

"Come out from under there," said Terry, pointing at Kyle.

Kyle shrugged and Terry mimed for him to pull out his earplugs.

"Stand up."

Crosby watched Kyle struggle to get out from under the desk and thought Kyle had done well to fold his gangly frame into such a small space in the first place.

"Who are you?" Terry asked

"I'm no one," said Kyle.

"What are you doing in here?"

"He's my son."

Terry turned to see Crosby crawl out from under an adjacent desk, hands raised in surrender.

"So, nepotism rules at Solarvecchi Zotte AI now, does it? CEO Bing is replacing us all with his son, is he?"

"He's not here to work, he's here to pick up his Christmas presents from me, only I couldn't find them."

A man Crosby recognised stepped out of the crowd who had paused when Crosby declared his presence.

"This the guy?" the man asked Terry who nodded.

The man approached Crosby, dressed all in brown, in what seemed like fancy dress, a tunic and tights and thin suede boots.

"It's time," the man declared.

The mob muttered until the man raised his hand.

"Get over there." Terry pointed both father and son in the direction of the desk by the window, Tamsin filming their every move on her phone.

"What have you done to Leni?" Crosby asked.

"He won't be causing us further problems," the man in the tunic said coldly.

"You told me I was in line for a promotion today, Bing," said Terry. "Told me I'd get an email around midday confirming it. I told my parents I was in line for good news. Even booked them a holiday cruise around the Caribbean to celebrate. You are one sick person to then send me an email making me redundant instead."

Crosby felt his son's eyes burning into him.

"You planned this all along, didn't you?" Terry continued. "Use my skills, develop the latest iteration, launch it, then lay off half the team that created it, so you get the glory. And the girl."

Terry smiled at Tamsin who continued filming. "We were the classic turkeys voting for Christmas, weren't we?"

"It wasn't like that."

"What was it like? Tell me what it was like, Bing." That was the fancy dress man.

Crosby shook his head. "Believe it or not, I know what you're going through right now, Terry."

Terry snorted. "You haven't got the first idea what I'm going through."

Crosby considered revealing everything he'd experienced, all the realities he'd lived, the ghost he'd talked to, but knew it would sound crazy and Terry wouldn't buy it anyway. And it wasn't something his son needed to hear either.

"We can talk about a solution," said Crosby. "About you coming back in the new year."

Terry looked to the others and frowned. "You sack me and then a few hours later, you want to give me my job back?"

"It was a mistake we shouldn't have made. I can see you're angry…"

"Angry? What did you expect, a party atmosphere? You've fired half of the creative department on Christmas Eve. Couldn't you have waited until the new year?"

"There are targets to meet. Shareholders and stakeholders to answer to. Efficiency savings to find."

"I found you those efficiency savings. The whole team did. And what's our reward? Sacrificing the jobs of half of us to help you make yet more efficiency savings. How many efficiency savings does a company need to make?"

"Companies would rather no people worked for them, so that all work can be pure profit, isn't that so?"

That was the tunic guy again. Crosby looked at him with disdain. "Who are you? Where's your party? We don't want to keep you."

A few gasps from the gathered group, like they weren't used to hearing this man criticised in any way.

"I appreciate the quips. But I represent a new movement. A fightback against your machines."

He raised a hand and one of his followers wielded an axe and smashed it into the nearest monitor."

"We're the Neo Luddites. You may have heard of us."

Crosby wanted to say that he had one of their leaflets in his pocket, but that was another reality, so he settled with a nod.

"We've had enough of your machines. It's time for a change."

Crosby couldn't help thinking why the ghost hadn't transitioned him here a little earlier in the day before those emails were sent. All of this could have been avoided.

"Come on," said Crosby, turning to Terry. "It's Christmas, you've all had a drink. Why don't we head back down the Anchor and I'll get a round in?"

The sound of another computer terminal meeting its end shattered the silence that followed what Crosby considered a very generous invitation to a group of people most of whom he'd never met before.

"No, no," said the Luddite leader. "The time for drinking is over."

"I've got my son with me. He's got to get to his Aunt's. Let's all go home to enjoy our Christmases, calm down a bit and come back and do this in January in the boardroom."

Smash. Another terminal gone. Crosby estimated about five grand in kit had been destroyed.

"How are any of us meant to enjoy Christmas without a job to come back to?" asked Terry. "I'd like to see you try that."

Again, Crosby was tempted to reveal all, about how he'd experienced exactly that kind of Christmas, but knew it wouldn't make sense.

"String him up," the Luddite leader ordered, his patience exhausted.

"Whay?" Crosby was genuinely shocked by the sudden change in tone and direction.

Three of the mob stepped forward, two grabbed Crosby, while one held a length of thick rope. Another smashed another workstation.

"No," Kyle yelled, striding toward his father before being blocked and surrounded by several burly drunks.

"Let my son go," said Crosby. "He's nothing to do with this. He doesn't have to see this."

"Everyone has to see this," vowed the Luddite. "This needs to go viral to serve as a warning to the world."

Kyle tried to shake himself free from his captors.

"Stay out of this, Kyle," said Crosby. "It's not your problem."

"You're my Dad," he said. "Despite all you've done. And not done."

Others in the mob pushed Kyle away from his father toward reception while another tied Crosby's hands behind his back.

"I hope you're capturing all this," said Terry, looking to Tamsin who gave him the thumb's up, phone held to her face.

Someone looped the rope around one of the exposed pipes that criss-crossed the office ceiling, tying one end into a noose.

"Are we still running?" the Luddite asked.

Tamsin nodded and the leader of the mob turned to face her.

"Dear world," he announced in a voice with calm authority, "the time has come for people to fight back. For too long recently, we've all been victims of the unrestricted spread of artificial intelligence that the makers themselves admit threatens the future of mankind. Today, myself and my fellow Neo Luddites are saying enough is enough. Because today, yet more people lost their jobs to machines. More people have been rendered useless and face losing their homes, their livelihoods. On Christmas Eve, people, a day that means so much to so many. But absolutely nothing to machines. It's time to serve notice that we refuse to bow down before technology."

Tamsin followed the Luddite with her camera as he moved across the office toward Crosby.

"Here we have someone who heads-up what is currently one of the most powerful and influential companies on the planet. This man has been responsible for the development of technology that has stolen thousands of jobs from humans. He is one of the few to make money out of this bringing misery to millions. And today, he sacked seven of his workforce who have all since repented for working in this discriminatory industry. Their jobs were lost all in the name of making efficiency savings.."

Tamsin panned up to show the noose dangling from on high, then down to Crosby who'd been moved into position below it. Two members of the mob lifted Crosby up onto the table under the swinging noose.

"Let it be known that we ask you to think twice about the effects of your work upon humanity."

The man gave the nod and someone slipped a black hood over Crosby's head.

"Any last words?" the Luddite asked him.

The response was a mumble and the leader was forced to give the nod for the hood to be removed.

"Any last words?" he repeated.

Crosby took in all the air he could and looked to his son who couldn't look him in the eye.

"It has always been our intention here to develop AI to help the world," said Crosby, addressing Tamsin's camera. "And though we initially thought that the technology could be used in partnership with humans to increase their, our efficiency, recent iterations have shown us that this tech is vastly superior to any human being and is therefore destined to replace them. Us. I'm sorry I, we didn't make this clearer earlier. I accept my fate with good grace, and advise all others developing job stealing AI to cease their work immediately. These guys are serious. As you are about to see." He turned away from the camera. "I love you Kyle, and I'm sorry for everything bad I did and everything good I didn't do. And Terry, I wanted to save your job but..."

"But?"

"Getting pressure from above. The powers that be."

"You're the CEO," said Terry. "There is no above. The powers that be happen to be you."

Crosby was check-mated. He was a pawn in king's clothing and his crown was about to slip. If he could, he would have gladly withdrawn that email and given everyone their job back right there and then. But that would no doubt cost those left behind, and his credibility as a CEO would be shot to pieces. You didn't have to be in the C-suite to know that U-turns are signs of weakness. You simply can't show weakness in business. Not if you want to survive.

"Just to confirm," said Terry, "you are getting machines in to replace us, the people you sacked today?"

Crosby had no idea of the board's plans of course, but it sounded about right, so he nodded. "I signed off the new iteration of the software two weeks ago. Software yourself and Tamsin developed, I believe. Plus the rest of you who lost your jobs today."

The heads of the accused dropped. "They have all repented," said the Luddite leader, who then turned his attention back to the camera. "And all those who turn away from the machines, despite what you have done, will be spared this fate."

"Except me, apparently," said Crosby. "Where's your humanity towards me?"

"You have released evil into the world. Evil that threatens to end the world. There is no way back for you."

"It's another gamechanger that will really put Solarvecchi Zotte AI on the map," said Crosby. "Create new jobs."

"And wipe thousands more jobs off the face of the planet in the process."

"We're just doing what everyone else is doing. If we don't keep up, we fall behind."

"Corporate bull and you know it," said Terry.

"It's sad to see so many humans siding with machines," said the Luddite. "Just out of interest, why do you prefer them to us?"

Crosby paused and looked at the faces staring at him from different points around the room. The other six who'd been sacked looked solemn, a few with eyes ringed red from tears, others with eyes glazed from drink and hearts emptied by fear for their future. A fear he was responsible for generating.

"It's not a case of preferring them, it's seeing the advantages," he said, mechanically.

"We're human, they're not. We need paying, they don't. We need breaks and holidays, they don't."

Crosby nodded at Terry. "I know. But when you see the spreadsheets, it's a no-brainer for businesses. The move to machines is going to happen eventually to pretty much everyone. Might as well start somewhere. Might as well be here and now."

The Luddite leader had heard enough and gave the nod for the hood to be replaced over Crosby's head.

A pair of hands dragged him closer to the noose, while another mob member jumped onto the adjacent table and pulled the noose down around Crosby's neck.

"Ghost, ghost," Crosby called out, his words muffled by the hood but clear enough to anyone standing within two metres.

"Help me, ghost. I've seen enough."

"No one helps those who turn against their own kind, who side with enemies just because that enemy offers them riches," said the Luddite leader. "You have profited from the misery of others."

"Ghost? I don't want this. I understand now."

As Tamsin filmed and Kyle looked on, the Luddite kicked away the table from under Crosby's feet.

Kyle screamed.

# Chapter 7:
## A resolution reeking of festive spirit

Crosby woke with a start. Felt himself restricted, a tie on, shirt, suit, smart shoes. He couldn't move. The room was dark, a figure dressed in black, head bowed at the foot of the bed, sobbing. The figure approached him, stooped to deliver a soft kiss on his forehead and was gone, quietly shutting the door on the way out.

"Ghost, ghost!" Crosby had to think the words for he could not speak them, the gift of speech taken from him like the gift of movement. But he could see the room, and he'd heard the sobbing.

Panic engulfed him as he remembered his fate in the office at the hands of the Luddites. The noose, the fall, the snap, the end.

"Ghost!"

"I am here."

"O, thank you. I'm alive?"

"No. Dead, and in your coffin. Quite an expensive one by the looks."

"Can you get me out of here?"

"You really didn't read that small print, did you?"

"No, no. Was there a bit about dying?"

"Of course, and you're fully covered. You just need to make a decision before they put you in the oven or the ground."

"I have to choose one of the three?"

"That was the deal. In the small print and everything, but let's not go there again."

"This one's out of the question."

"I thought you'd say that."

"And in the one before I face a long prison sentence."

"A good twelve years at least I'd say."

"So that leaves the first, where I'm sleeping rough."

"Quite."

"What about a fourth option."

"Fourth?"

"Can I go back to where I started?"

The ghost exhaled. "That's definitely not in the small print."

"Come on. It must be an option."

"It's a little uncouth, I must say, but in your case understandable, given the sheer awfulness of all three realities. I've never seen such a terrible trio, I must admit. Everyone usually goes for the last option, which is usually so beneficial. That's why it's the last of the three. Less work for us to do to transport you back to one of the other realities."

"Death is not for me."

"You're sure? You seemed quite keen on it before, that's what brought me here in the first place."

"I've had a rethink. Even though my original situation is far from ideal, it's better than all the others. It's the one in which we're all together, in the house, me, Marie and Kyle."

"Well, you're all in the house together now. Marie and Kyle are downstairs."

"Yes. But I'm upstairs and dead in a coffin."

"There is that."

"Can you do it? Can you get me back?"

"Don't see why not?"

"Will things be exactly the same as I left them?"

"Like none of this ever happened."

"But I'll remember the other realities?"

"You'll remember the lessons you needed to learn from them."

"That's good enough for me."

The ghost exhaled. "So that's it. Decision made."

Crosby tried to sit up before remembering he was dead. "I have to thank you for what you've done. You've shown me the light and the error of my ways."

"While most ghosts frighten the life out of you, I like to think I've frightened the life back into you."

"I am still dead, I believe."

"Ah yes, best sort that out for you."

Crosby waited, heard the ghost whisper, "Goodbye, Nicholas. And good luck," and closed his eyes.

He woke to find himself still lying on a soft surface in a dark room.

"Oh, no," he thought. The ghost couldn't transition him back.

Then he felt his chest move. His mouth exhale. His forefinger on his left hand flick the duvet. His right foot jolt.

Slowly he sat up. He was on his mahogany bed in his bedroom. One bedpost missing, lying by the wardrobe.

He peered under the bed and saw discarded wrapping paper. Slowly got up and walked round to the other side of the bed and opened the bedside cabinet and pulled out the box, a receipt wrapped around it.

He quickly re-wrapped the gift, fastening the ribbon and replaced the whole package in the cabinet.

Back to the other side of the bed where he checked the folds of his brown shirt hanging over the wardrobe door, then picked up the make-up sponge from Marie's dressing table and examined it closely. No signs of life. Or death.

He caught his reflection in the mirror, still wearing his office shirt and trousers, a few hours of stubble growth salt and peppering his jaw.

Back from the dead, he said to himself, considering, quite rightly, that perhaps that ought not to be the sort of thing one said out loud in any circumstances.

There's people way worse off than you, Crosby, he then said to himself. Nobody knows how many Christmases they have left, so make the most of every one. Starting with this one.

Crosby checked his knuckles and found no sign of redness. Ran his fingers around his neck – no break, no soreness, just a little more stubble growth.

Oh, yeah, and you've got a pretty mean punch on you, apparently, which you should use on yourself if you don't make this one of the best Christmases your family has ever had.

He quietly opened the bedroom door, the light from the living room downstairs bouncing off the staircase walls. He crept across the landing to the spare room, pushed open the door and flicked on the light. He rarely entered his wife's studio, not that she minded him going in, just that he liked to keep it as her special space. The easel in its centre held a canvas that looked like it had started out as a portrait but had been covered by angry brush strokes in brown and red. The painted scrawl contrasted with the delicate colours and detailed observations of Marie's earlier works on the walls, beautiful and brighter portraits in which she'd captured a real likeness of her sitters: two of Kyle, one of her sister Karla and a self-portrait. Did it bother Crosby that none were of him?

Cards on the table: It rankled a little, and he had a good idea why. She had tried before but never liked the outcome. Said when she painted him all she seemed to commit to canvas was a dark, somewhat evil version of him.

He punched a message into his phone before going downstairs. When he reached the living room, the silver and black of the television screen and the multi-colour of the Christmas tree lights and the searing silver of the tinsel decorations coloured the walls cosy. Marie and Kyle were watching a black and white Basil Rathbone as *Sherlock Holmes* thriller.

Crosby sat down on the sofa next to his wife, amazed and grateful to see her alive.

"Feel better now?" she asked.

Crosby nodded. "Sorry about earlier, both of you."

"Forget it," said Marie, not looking anywhere except at the screen. "Can't be nice losing your job."

"Can't be nice what's happening to you and your job, either," he said. She turned to look him in the eye. "I mean it," he continued. "I can see why you're annoyed at what the machines are doing to the art world."

"Are you feeling alright?"

"Never better."

"Let's not get into this now," she said.

He nodded. "I'll do my best to make amends," he whispered to her.

Kyle faced his father from the armchair and offered a smile. His son looked like the innocent that he'd last seen in the stationers at the station that morning. He preferred him like this, not too smartly attired, but by no means scruffy. And home. Not off to stay with his aunt or hang out in the park. Home with his mum and dad, drinking orange juice, not alcohol.

"Come on," Crosby said, knowing the film was finishing as the classical soundtrack reached its crescendo. "We're going out."

Both of them looked at him in shock.

"What?"

"I'm not going on a train again," said Marie.

"No, me neither," said Crosby. "We're getting a cab. Come on, get ready. We're going to the restaurant."

"But our booking was two hours ago. I've got stuff in the freezer we could have."

"Save it for another time. We may need it. In the meantime, we've got a tradition to uphold."

In the cab on the way up to London, they counted the Christmas lights in the houses. It didn't matter to Crosby that the rain was light and the traffic heavy. He was with the two most important people in his life and determined to make them happy.

"We used to just count the trees," said Crosby.

"What, back in that black and white Christmas of 1881?" mocked Kyle.

"1981, cheeky. Do you remember it, Maz?"

"I wasn't even born. We're not all as ancient as you, remember."

Crosby took the jibe in good grace and wiped a clearing in the cab window's condensation. "There's more lights than trees these days. I remember just counting the trees. Then those candles in arrowhead formation became popular and we counted those too. Now there's so many different lights and shapes."

"It's called progress, Dad."

"Progress isn't always beneficial though, is it?" He squeezed Marie's hand.

"You're going to moan about the commercialisation of Christmas in a minute, aren't you?" joked Marie.

"Well. It has gotten a bit corporate around the edges, hasn't it? Ever since they made Santa wear red."

"Whose fault's that?"

Crosby's thoughts turned to the job he'd lost, the regular income he'd used to rely on. The fact that it was gone lit a flicker of fear deep in his gut, something he knew he'd have to live with awhile until he sorted things out. But worse than that, more pressing than that, there was a full-on flame of fear inside him that he had to extinguish that very night so that he could sleep well and enjoy Christmas Day.

La Spatchas had received Crosby's request for a rearranged sitting and the trio sat at a table designed for two but just big enough for three.

"Order whatever you like," said Crosby. "Don't spare the horses."

"They're not on the menu, are they?" Kyle looked around the table, pleased with his quip and the smiling reaction it got from his parents.

"I'm going for the winter vegetable to start with," said Crosby, his wife nodding in agreement.

Nothing of import happened during the act of eating, except that when the soup was done, the door to the restaurant opened and a smartly dressed kid about Kyle's age held it open for a older man, who strode in with purpose and headed for one of the private booths without acknowledging any of the members of staff. Crosby recognised the guy as the CEO of Solarvecchi Zotte AI who'd never said hello to him before and clearly wasn't about to make an exception to that habit now, having signed off his sacking earlier in the day.

Being seated behind him, Crosby was unable to watch them during the meal, but he had an inkling of how awkward the conversation would be, and overheard only this toward the end of the meal:

"Just come back to the office, I'll find the presents."

"But it's late, Dad. I've been waiting around all day."

"Business doesn't stop being business just because it's Christmas Eve, son. Now, what you having for dessert?"

Ten minutes later, the CEO and his son left before Crosby had settled up, the top brass walking past Crosby's table without a hint of recognition of his employee. That got Crosby wondering if he'd blanked someone from Solarvecchi Zotte AI when he'd walked out with his son.

"Shall we take a walk up to Regent Street to see the lights?" he suggested to Marie and Kyle when they got outside, having tipped the waitress generously, but not excessively.

"How far is it?" Kyle asked, not unfairly.

"It's about a mile to Oxford Street then a little way after that."

Kyle shrugged and hooked his arm into his mother's who had an inkling why Crosby wanted to walk that way.

They passed crouching beggars holding forth polystyrene coffee cups. Crosby stopped and stooped to slip a five pound note into the cups of the first five unfortunates he encountered, apologising to the rest that he was out of change. This prompted the remaining beggars to produce their card readers, against which Crosby tapped his credit card, donating five pounds to each and all.

'Merry Christmas, sir," one called out as Crosby rejoined his wife and son, both of whom looked shocked.

Sure enough, when they reached the outside of the modest Solarvecchi Zotte AI building, just six storeys high, Crosby stopped.

"I just want to say a proper goodbye to Leni, the door guy. Why don't you two keep walking. I'll catch you up. Just keep heading straight. I'll find you."

"Are you going to take a leak on the big boss' desk?" Kyle asked.

"I've just been."

"What about a number two?"

"Kyle!" His mother playfully slapped him.

Crosby handed Marie a twenty. "Get yourselves a coffee on the way."

Marie shrugged, took the money and they walked off as Crosby walked in, Leni smiling and ending his call early, standing and walking out from behind his desk to embrace Crosby.

"I'm so sorry about what happened."

Crosby smiled. "Not your fault."

"It such terrible time for this news. Just before Christmas."

"He just went up, didn't he?"

Leni grimaced and nodded. "In the lift with his son."

"Do you think I could go up there?"

Leni grimaced again. "I'm under strict orders, Nick, not to allow any of you up there."

"Why don't you come up with me?"

Leni checked his watch and smiled. "I suppose that wouldn't hurt. You need to pick up the present for your kid too, huh?"

Crosby nodded and after Leni had locked the entrance door they took the stairs, side by side, past the floor on which the HR department plied their dubious trade and onto the creative floor. The lights were on in reception, but the door was locked. Of course, Leni had keys.

"He'll hear us coming in, won't he?" Leni asked, looking a little worried, like a school kid entering a room he knew was out of bounds.

"I doubt it."

Leni held the door open for Crosby who headed straight through reception to his old desk, facing the window, next to Terry's.

He checked his watch. Anytime now.

He stood and glanced out of the window, down on High Holborn, Marie and Kyle surely safely out of the area by now.

They didn't have long to wait for the smash of glass from street level to echo up the stairs from reception.

"What the…?" Leni cried out, looking first at Crosby, then out of the window.

They both rushed through reception onto the stairwell and saw the drunken mob below surging into the building.

"What the…"

"We should go back in there," Crosby suggested.

"But it's my job to…"

Crosby grabbed his arm and looked him in the eye. "Your life's way more important."

Leni felt torn but nodded and followed Crosby back into the reception. The CEO had come out to investigate.

"What's going on?" he asked. "What's he doing in here?" he said pointing at Crosby. "And what are you doing here?" he then said, glaring at Leni.

"You need to get out of here," said Crosby. "This could turn nasty."

"What could turn nasty? Who is it?"

"At a rough guess, I'd say it's a drunken mob containing a few, if not all of the people you made redundant earlier today minus me, plus a few bloodthirsty Luddites looking to go viral."

"Luddites?" The CEO frowned at the specific nature of his reply. "Where's security?" he demanded.

"They're part of the mob."

"What?"

"I suspect you made them work all day today, right?"

"That's what they're paid to do. It's not a public holiday. The wheels need to keep on turning. If they don't like it, it won't be long before we get a machine to do their jobs. Then they can stay in the pub for as long as they like."

"Whatever."

"I'll call the police on them."

"You can try, but it's busy with last minute shoppers out there. They won't get here in time."

"In time for what? What do these people want?"

"Your head on a plate."

"What?"

"Let's be honest, the work we do here, well, the work I used to do here before you sacked me on Christmas Eve... It's…it's anti-human isn't?"

"What are you talking about?"

"We're developing tech that's taking people's jobs away."

"It's a tired old argument I'm quite frankly fed up of hearing."

The roar from the staircase got louder.

Leni gripped his keys, thinking they might make a decent weapon. The CEO's son looked to his father.

"I didn't want to come back here in the first place," he said, on the verge of tears. "If you hadn't forgotten my presents, I'd be halfway home by now."

"I've still no idea where they are, I'm sorry, but we have more pressing problems right now."

"I'm scared, father."

"That's the wine talking. It's making you emotional. You should have stuck to water."

Crosby turned to the CEO. "Are you going to hang around and tell these people that they shouldn't be angry about what AI is doing to the world?"

The CEO looked flustered, checked his watch. "I… er… we have a table booked. But I'll certainly be having words with them."

"Leni," said Crosby. "Would you mind showing these two gentlemen the way out, please? You have the keys to the emergency exit by the kitchen?"

"Of course. But what about you?"

"If you don't mind, I'd like to clear my desk, relive a few old memories and find my son's Christmas present."

The CEO didn't look happy about the arrangement, even less happy about the approaching mob.

"Go, quickly, now," said Crosby. "And Merry Christmas."

Leni turned and smiled a thumbs up, as did the CEO's son, but there was nothing from the top brass. There never was.

Crosby fired up his machine, opened up the file entitled 'Latest Iteration' on his desktop.

"Oi! I know you're in here." Terry's voice echoed across the open plan office as did his fist hitting the door. A few thumps and kicks later, the door was down, the mob was in, and the lights were on.

"Bing?"

Crosby swung his chair around to face Terry, who was joined by people he recognised as fellow former employees, camera operator Tamsin, and the guy in the brown tunic who'd ordered his execution in the previous reality.

"Is this him?" the Luddite leader asked.

"What are you doing, Bing? How did you get back in? We had to break in."

"I heard. I've got friends in low places."

"Leni let you in?"

"Of course. And guess what I've been up to?"

Terry's eyes widened. "You haven't?"

Crosby smiled. "Just need you to keep your half of the bargain within the next eight minutes and thirty-six seconds."

"What about the top brass boy? Someone said they saw him come back in here?"

Crosby shrugged. "He never once paid any attention to me. Don't see why I would him."

Terry rushed across the office and sat at his workstation next to Crosby's.

"Let's get the team back together one last time," he said, smiling.

Crosby nodded as the other invaders gathered behind them.

"Who's the guy in the tunic?" he whispered to Terry.

"What guy in the tunic?" Terry asked.

Crosby looked round and scanned the group watching them. No guy in any tunic. He rubbed his neck.

"What are you two doing?" Tamsin asked.

Crosby and Terry looked at each other then back at their screens.

"As the designers and programmers of Solarvecchi Zotte AI tech, there are certain failsafe mechanisms we decided to put in place without the top brass knowing," Crosby said.

"Certain self-destruct features shall we say?" Terry added, typing a few words that resulted in his machine making a few beeps and a 'Ready to Disable' message flashing up on screen.

# Chapter 8:
## In which normality returns, kind of

Crosby walked west toward the lights of Regent Street, head held high in the failing daylight, the bright multi-colours of the Christmas street decorations bringing joy. He met with Marie and Kyle in the coffee shop, they having bought him a tea and they sat amid the throng of the excited and the excitable, looking forward to the exceptional days to come where people would meet and presents be exchanged.

The taxi home was again spent counting lights, with more to enjoy as older people hunkered down for a night of cracking walnuts in front of pretty decent television, while the younger prepared for a night out with friends in pubs, clubs and bars.

Back at home, Kyle stayed up until just gone eleven, still a little excited about the day to come, even though he knew Santa would not be paying a visit.

Marie told Crosby she felt a little old now their son was no longer a believer which Crosby totally understood.

"Maybe I could sit for you in the new year," he said, after pouring them both a sherry from a bottle they'd bought years ago and only drunk from in December.

She looked at him with surprise.

"Now I'll have a bit more time," he added.

"Aren't you scared I'll expose the darkness in your soul?" she asked.

"What's there is there," he said. "But I feel something's lifted. Something's changed. Maybe that will come through in what you paint this time."

"Who knows? What are your plans for work?" she asked.

"I'll look for a new job in January. Something completely new."

"Not the same business?"

He shook his head. "I'm finished with that world, now. Time to move on."

Marie smiled a little but knew him leaving that world would not mean an end to that world. The threat to her livelihood remained strong from the art machines, but growing unrest within the community would hopefully see the dial flick back in the favour of the genuinely talented and creative in the new year, and away from the frauds, scrapists and talentless that used AI.

Of course, Crosby knew that no immediate change would be forthcoming from what he and Terry had done. Solarvecchi Zotte AI's new iteration would certainly fail, the code scrambled. It would cost the business its new clients, its reputation, its CEO his bonus, which is why Tamsin had to be held back by the Luddites in the office when she realised the implications of what he and Terry were doing.

But it was for the best. Crosby knew Tamsin would have no trouble finding alternative employment in one of the growing number of businesses founded on using AI trained on the works of talented artists and writers without their permission. Another name, another business would fill the void left by Solarvecchi Zotte AI, and Tamsin would continue to have no qualms about taking home ill-gotten gains made by profiting from the misery of millions.

Crosby excused himself from the lounge to head upstairs and bring the presents down, telling Marie to stay snug on the sofa as he'd sort it all.

When he was done, he sat next to his wife, slipping his arm around her shoulder. She let her head tip to rest on his shoulder and took a deep breath.

Printed in Great Britain
by Amazon